D0767470

F/2037202

We're All in This Together

A Novella

Owen King

faber and faber

First published in 2006
by Faber and Faber Limited
3 Queen Square London WC1N 3AU
Published in the United States by Bloomsbury USA

Printed in England by Mackays of Chatham Ltd

A CIP record for this book
is available from the British Library

ISBN 978-0-571-22724-2

ISBN 0-571-22724-4

2 4 6 8 10 9 7 5 3 1

For Kelly,
the prettiest girl in Yuma

Reports that say that something hasn't happened are always interesting to me, because as we know, there are known knowns; there are things we know we know. We also know there are known unknowns; that is to say we know there are some things we do not know. But there are also unknown unknowns—the ones we don't know we don't know. And if one looks throughout the history of our country and other free countries, it is the latter category that tend to be the difficult ones.

—Donald Rumsfeld on the question of
Iraq and WMDs, February 12, 2002

We're All in This Together

DON'T MOURN!

When you are a kid, adults are always telling you about their revelation, the moment when the mist cleared and they saw what it was they wanted, or finally understood what it was that never made sense before.

For instance, my grandfather told me that he decided to be a union organizer after he saw the man who lived next door at the boarding-house come home one morning after a late shift at the paper mill, remove his shoes at the door, and pass them off to his wife, who then slipped them on and continued out on her way to another job. As the man handed off his shoes, my grandfather realized that what the man was actually handing off was his dignity, and that a life without dignity was no different from a life without love—because how could a man without dignity bear to love another person, when he must hate himself so much?

Dr. Vic claimed that he fell in love with my mother when he looked out his office window one sunny afternoon to see her striding up to the elderly Catholic priest who sometimes prayed on the sidewalk in front of the Planned Parenthood office for hours at a time. The old priest appeared to be swaying slightly; Emma helped him from his knees over to a bench. After that, she went back inside, and came out a minute later with a cold bottle of water for the holy man. Dr. Vic watched it all, and wondered how many times that old crank had warned my mother that she was on the path to hell, and there she was anyhow, doing the decent thing to save him from a case of sunstroke, or worse. Until then I only thought she was beautiful, said Dr. Vic, but that proved it.

At a rally for striking longshoremen in Portland, my grandmother said she heard Papa relate the story about his neighbors who had to share a single pair of shoes, and while she felt compelled by his words, she didn't fully devote herself to the cause until after the meeting—when he came down from the platform and shook her hand. Nana had seen other union men talk, and dramatically whip off their coats, and stomp around in their braces while they railed against the bosses. She even met one of these big stomping sorts once, and it was like shaking hands with a liver. When she was introduced to my grandfather, though, Nana realized immediately that Papa was different: in spite of his suit, my grandfather wasn't a college boy, or a politician—he was an actual stevedore, just like her brother and her uncle. She could tell this by the fine dirt in the creases beneath his eyes, what her mother used to call "Working Man's Scars." Then Papa stuck out his hand, said, "How do," and Nana grasped it. He had clean hands, dry hands. She was moved to think of how hard he had worked to get himself clean. Finally, she thought, here was a young man who believed in something.

What I take from these stories is the impression that until that certain moment—the awakening, the sign—each of us is waiting outside the life that we are meant for, like a stranger with nothing to do but sit on the steps until the Realtor arrives. Then she does appear, charging up the walk, a fury of possibility and jingling keys. She throws open the door, and hurries you inside, and you know, right then. This is the place, the one place you really belong.

Except, I think now that for most people, it's more complex than that. In the moment of realization, maybe the mist doesn't actually clear, but thicken, taking on color, smell, and taste. Maybe the house is for sale because it's haunted; maybe every house is haunted.

When Papa saw the man give his wife the pair of shoes, he saw that something was wrong, but maybe he summed too quickly, and underestimated the depth of a man's dignity. When my mother brought the old priest a bottle of water, maybe Dr. Vic bet too high on Emma's generosity, and too low on the hard-earned pessimism of *a single mother and motivated activist, who undoubtedly worried a good deal more about the news stories that would follow the death of a priest on the sidewalk in front of the clinic, than she ever did about the man actually dying. And was there ever a time—years and years after she took the clean hand of the dirty soapboxer that day on the docks—that my grandmother wondered just what my grandfather's effort amounted to, now that they lived in a time and in a place where it seemed that the filthiest thing you could say about a person was that they were liberal, that they had a bleeding heart?*

Obviously, something was on Nana's mind when she died. After January, she never again left the guest bedroom, and one morning in early March, I found her cold. A sour, ponderous expression lay on her face, a grimace of real dissatisfaction, as if she had been expecting a surprise, but just maybe not the one she received. Her eyes were open, too, and fixed on the framed portrait of Joseph Hillstrom that hung on the wall.

In those last seconds, what did she see in the eyes of labor's truest martyr? Did she see the cool expression of a sincere organizer? Or did she see the passionless stare of a killer?

Four months later, in the middle of summer, and with the grass already grown full and burnt brown on Nana's grave, I saw something that surprised me, too. At the time, I understood it couldn't be real, that it was a hallucination. But, these days, I know better than to believe my eyes. Sometimes up really is down; sometimes the ground is the water, and the sky is a cliff.

In the morning, before setting out, I eat a bowl of oatmeal and write my mother a quick note. Have a lovely day with your conscience. *There's nothing unusual about this; my mother and I are regular correspondents. Without knocking, I stride into the bathroom while she is in the shower and smack the yellow legal pad against the frosted glass so she can read it. I record her silence, the trickle of water down the drain, and the squeaking of her feet, as a minor victory.*

When I roll my bike out of the garage, Dr. Vic sticks his head out the window of his BMW and asks if I want a lift on his way to work.

"Sorry, but I don't take rides from strange men," I say. I usher my mother's fiancé on his way with a sweeping gesture.

Dr. Vic responds to my challenge with perfect, maddening acquiescence: he gives a pleasant nod, and simply coasts down the driveway, when any normal person would slam on the gas and lay down a patch of screw-you-kid rubber.

But I am feeling good as I pedal out onto Route 12, heading for the tall white house on Dundee Avenue where my mother grew up and Nana died. The wind and the summer smells of grass and tar make me feel fast, and on that markerless stretch of road I can pretend I am between almost any two places in the world. Leaving always gives me a high feeling, and the bad part—the coming back—is a whole day away. Route 12 dips and rises. I lean into a bend and the first sign of town comes into view. The Beachcomber, a beleaguered ranch motel, crouches across from the mouth of the interstate ramp, catering to late-night drivers who are too tired to make it south to Boston, or north to Bangor and Canada.

That's when I see it—see them. I glance at the motel and there are three men standing on the boardwalk in front of a room, loading the trunk of a taxi. There is nothing distinct about these men: they are all white; they all appear to be in the normal range of weight and build; they are all dressed in suits and ties. In other words, they are three men, three normal men, boarding a taxi. The taxi is a member of the local fleet, a creaky-looking station wagon with plastic wood panels.

When the trio climbs in, I observe the undercarriage of the cab sag slightly beneath their collective mass. Then I am around the corner and turning into town.

I pass another block before I apprehend very clearly what it is that was so striking about the three strangers: that is, the three men weren't strangers at all. Those men were my mother's old boyfriends. They were Paul and Dale and Jupps, all of them, together. In another block, I work out the many reasons why this is not possible, not the least of which happens to be that none of my mother's boyfriends ever knew each other. Besides, Paul lives way up north, and this is tourist season, his busy time, and as far as we know, Jupps didn't even live in the United States anymore. On top of that, the only time I could ever recall having seen any of them wearing a tie was Dale at Nana's funeral, and that had been a bow tie.

No, of course not. Of course, I didn't see them.

What I saw didn't even qualify as a hallucination; it was too boring. My vision was more like some kind of sad little kid wish, like an imaginary friend, or your Real Father. Not the crazy drunk that your mother's ex-boyfriend once had to beat the shit out of with a snow shovel, not the jerk-off felon who never gave you anything in your whole life except a polydactyl toe and a five-dollar bill for your tenth birthday—not him, not that imposter—but your Real Father, the superhero. Your Real Father is sorry to have put you through all this, but he couldn't risk it, because if his enemies ever discovered his secret identity, his family would have been in terrible danger. But now everything can be different—because he needs your help—and the invisible spy plane is idling in a grassy field outside of town and it's go, go, go! The fate of the world may depend on it!

In the time it takes to consider the matter logically and, in turn, dust off the old (but not that old) Real Father Fantasy, I have traveled another two blocks. I have also started to cry. I slam on the brakes and start back to the motel, standing on the pedals and pushing uphill. But the gravel parking lot is empty; the men and the taxi are somewhere up the road, out of sight.

I am still sniffling when I reach my grandparents' house and find a small gathering in the front yard. My grandfather and the neighbors, Gil Desjardins and his wife, Mrs. Desjardins, stand before the 15 × 15-foot billboard that Papa has recently posted on the lawn, and which lists, succinctly, his deeply felt political beliefs concerning the most recent election, between Al Gore and George W. Bush.

I roll onto the grass and pull up beside them. Between their shoulders I make out slashes of pink paint, and even before reading the latest accusation, the situation is evident: for the third time in a month, the vandal, the fascist paperboy, Steven Sugar, has attacked.

"Somehow," says Gil, "that the paint is pink, that makes it worse, doesn't it?"

Mrs. Desjardins flicks away a pink chip with her fingernail. She clucks sympathetically.

Papa crosses his arms and contemplates the pink message in silence.

Mrs. Desjardins purses her lips at me and gives my bicep a squeeze. She wears a kimono and a thin black ribbon fastened around her old woman's neck. It is accepted that Gil's wife is odd.

"Whoever would have guessed a bourgeois newspaper could lead to such a rumpus?" Her gaze falls on me expectantly.

I shrug.

"Oh, for shit's sake, Lana," says Gil.

"It is bourgeois. The New York Times *is bourgeois."*

"That may be, but if you say 'bourgeois,' you sound like an asshole. In fact, I've been told that 'bourgeois' is a code word that assholes use to recognize each other when they're in unfamiliar places. If you even spell it in Scrabble, it makes you sound like an asshole."

"I believe you're being obtuse again, Gilbert," she says, not sounding displeased.

At the center of the group, Papa has hardly shifted. I see now that what the vandal has sprayed across the billboard this time is the inexplicable—and yet, somehow, terribly damning—epithet **COMMUNIST SHITHEEL.** Papa reaches out and uses his knuckle to trace the letter C. The thin-lipped expression on his face is unreadable. "It's enough to make a person think—" he starts, and lets the thought hang.

My grandfather gently moves his knuckle around the letter O.

"Well, Henry, don't kill yourself. I'm going home to read the dictionary and try to take a piss."

Gil starts scraping his walker back in the direction of his house. When he reaches the edge of the driveway, he encounters some difficulty in trying to jerk the legs over the lip of the pavement, and I rush over to help. He throws his arm over my shoulder and I guide the walker up onto the driveway.

"Thanks, George," he says, pausing to catch his breath. Then, seeming less to speak to me than to himself, "Man's too old to get wound up like this. Especially over this. As if there's any real *difference between the two of them. One's a fool from Tennessee who wants to tell us how to live, and the other's a damn fool from Texas who wants to tell us how to live. Either way, we were going to end up with a fool. No difference." He crutches down to the sidewalk, his wife beside him and rubbing his back. They disappear around the hedge.*

I return to my grandfather. With his palm pressed gently against the billboard, he looks almost prayerful, not unlike the photograph in a recent newsmagazine I have happened to see, of a penitent at the Wailing Wall in Israel.

"Papa," I say. I feel a sudden need to be reassured that I am not crazy. If there is anyone who can explain what I saw—what I thought I saw—it is Papa. "On the way here, I was on my bike, and I saw this cab . . ."

He turns and blinks at me.

Until now, I suddenly realize, Papa has not even been aware of my presence, does not even realize that the Desjardins have left, maybe doesn't even know they were here in the first place. Which is why, when he sees me now, sees my raw eyes and flushed cheeks, Papa construes their meaning in the only way that must seem possible to him.

The old man steps forward and embraces me, hard. "Don't worry, George," he says, "the paint will come off."

I open my mouth, close it.

We spend an hour soaking the pink paint off the billboard, and then my grandfather and I drive to the sporting goods store and browse until we find the right weapon.

1.

For armor, I went looking in the junk closet in my grandparents' garage. When I opened the door a cascade of twenty-year-old Halloween decorations and disassembled fishing poles poured out, along with a lot of other interesting things: moth-eaten life preservers, sheaves of ancient AFL-CIO newsletters wilted up like onion skins, a few ratty lures, a tire gauge with a cracked face, a Richard Nixon mask. I sat on a milk crate and put the mask on my hand, made it talk to me. I was in no hurry. "Maybe he'll just forget," said Tricky Dick. "McGlaughlins have long memories," I said. "But you're a Claiborne," said Dick, "I recognize you by the devilish toe." This surprised and silenced me. I sat in the cool dark of the garage and tried to think of some silly song for Nixon to sing. Maybe he had really forgotten, maybe he had come to his senses, I thought, but a moment later, through the wall, I heard the old man's voice calling for me.

I sighed, shook off the mask, and dug the softball equipment out from the bottom of the closet, a too big chest protector and a pair of cracked shin guards that reeked of mold. There was, however, no catcher's mask and no jock.

Around the back of the house, on the patio, I reported to my grandfather.

"Well, there's nothing to be done about it," he said. "I'll just have to aim low."

Papa was stoned, and eating peanuts. He took one salty piece at a time, rolling it between his fingertips, and finally plopping the peanut into his mouth. The automatic rifle lay balanced across the arms of his deck chair.

Gil, who besides living next door was also my grandfather's best friend, made a disapproving noise from the back of his throat. He was attempting to fire the black stub of a roach held in a twisted paper clip, flicking a lighter and sucking wetly.

My grandfather made an impatient hand-it-over gesture. This elicited another critical grunt, but then Gil passed over the works.

The afternoon, bright and dry, spun with pollen and carried the sound of children screaming from the public pool. Nearby, the five-hundred-shot ammo boxes were stacked up in a pyramid, like a display of beer cases at the supermarket. I put a hand in the pocket of my shorts and checked my package for reassurance.

Papa thumbed the light and drew deeply. The joint hissed to life, and he exhaled with relish. He raised a gray eyebrow at me. The corner of one bloodshot eye twitched. "What's the problem?"

I shifted my weight from foot to foot and tried to formulate a response that didn't sound too cowardly. The chest protector sagged around my torso. When I imagined being shot at, I saw myself running in circles, faster and faster, until my evasive maneuvers had gained the impossible quality of an accelerated film reel, and I was like a fool in a silent movie, doing a hotfoot jig on a bed of firecrackers. Then, an instant later, I saw myself take a direct hit in the sack, and plummet to the ground in a boneless heap, dead, balls pulverized.

I decided to abandon any pretence of courage. "Why don't you shoot at Gil, Papa?"

"With that walker? He's too slow."

"Thanks, kid."

"I said, 'I'll aim low.'" His eye was still twitching.

"High or low, Henry, it seems to me that the boy has ample reason for concern. His face and his ball bag are exposed.

"Your prudence is well earned, George." My grandfather's best friend waited a moment before adding an afterthought: "If it is wrong to be prudent about one's ball bag, then I, for one, would rather not be right." To punctuate this declaration, he threw me a wink and, simultaneously, stuck his hand under his armpit and squeezed off a long, wheezing fart.

Years ago, Gil had been an important official, a psychology professor and a dean at the university. Now he was just an old man, dying with uncommonly good cheer.

In his time, my grandfather, Henry McGlaughlin, had been an important official, too: the president for thirty years of Local 219. At a single word, he was capable of shutting down the Amberson Ironworks, and leaving the skeleton of an aircraft carrier shrouded on a dock for months, like a rich man's summer sloop. Of course, that too had been years ago, and now he was an old man, as well— but dying more slowly than his friend, and with no cheer to speak of.

I was fifteen years old and I wanted badly to please my grandfather, but I was a clumsy, unhappy boy, and I put little stock in the concept of trust, and none at all in faith. In the last few months my world had come to feel like a suit that I put on backward. Dr. Vic had offered me his opinion that this was all a phase—"a life passage," he called it—and that when I emerged, I would be a man. I asked Dr. Vic when he expected to emerge from his life passage. It took him a minute, but then he slapped his knee and said that was a good one.

Papa thrust the paper clip back to Gil. "Here, Gilbert. Stick this in your mouth."

When my grandfather turned back to me, his eyes were suddenly watery with feeling. "We're in this together, George," he said. "That's the thing."

This was a way of saying that we were a union of two, and in a union, you stood up for the next guy and you never broke ranks and you faced down the bosses and the finks and the goon squads with a solid front. "We're all in this together"; it was the essential promise that an organizer made to the workingmen who risked the livelihood of their families in an action. If another guy's family was hungry, you gave them half of what you had. If another guy came up short on his rent, you turned out your pockets. If another guy needed a hand, you reached out.

Here, in this place, Papa needed my help to confront a fink, a young fascist and vandal named Steven Sugar. And I needed somewhere to go, a safe place.

"Together," he repeated, and clasped his hands to show what the word meant.

I knew this was a practiced gesture, a piece of his old soapbox rally, but I couldn't doubt it.

If another guy needed a hand, you reached out.

So I went back to the garage, padded my crotch with a pair of athletic socks, pulled the Richard Nixon mask over my face, and stuck a southwester on my head. Then I ran back and forth in the sun for an hour while my grandfather tried to shoot me full of holes.

Separated by a distance of a hundred feet or so, Papa blasted at me from his position on the patio while I scrambled in and out of the stand of trees at the edge of the backyard. As the paintballs whizzed through the air above and around me, they tattered the leaves and burst against the trees with sharp, wet smacks. He yelled at me to stop moving so fast and play the part right, but I pretended not to hear. I only ran faster, spooked by the champagne pop of the rifle, cedar chips crunching beneath my feet, ozone hanging in the air, paint-stained branches slapping against my back. I ran until I was drenched through and seeing black spots out of Richard Nixon's eyeholes.

Then I heard Papa curse. That was enough, he called out. God-dammit that was enough.

I stayed in the trees until he finished unscrewing the automatic rifle from the tripod and tossed it to the ground with a thud. According to the sporting goods salesman this particular weapon, an IL-47, was the top of the line in paintball assault weapons; the IL stood for "Illustrator."

I emerged from the trees with my hands up. "I'm unarmed."

"Don't be a smartass."

Asleep in his lawn chair, Gil sat with his legs spread wide and a wet spot on the front of his pajamas. In the sun, his bald head was the color of skim milk, so pallid it hinted at blue. My grandfather had told me that the cancer was all through him, the way it had been with Nana toward the end. To me, that phrase, "all through him," described an image of the disease as a growth of black vines, twined around Gil's bones, thickening and choking, getting tighter and tighter, until eventually something would snap and that would be it.

After I shrugged off the catcher's equipment and hung Richard Nixon's sweaty face on the fence to dry, I went to Gil and shook him to make sure he was still alive.

He blinked several times, noted with only passing interest the dampness at his crotch, then looked around at the yard. "Looks like somebody got murdered out here. Murdered bad."

The yard did appear truly gruesome, as if someone had been knifed in the neck and then staggered around dramatically for hours, spouting from an endless reservoir of candy apple red arterial blood. There was paint all over the stand of larch trees, the boles and the branches and the leaves; paint on the patch of wild rhubarb and on the back fence; paint on the grass and on the dirt; paint on the igloo-

shaped birdhouse, as if a tiny Inuit had exploded; and even on the
pool, where an errant paintball had dissolved into a small pink slick.

Gil grunted himself up into his walker and clicked forward for a
closer look. He stopped and peered at the scummy surface of the
water. The pink slick drifted slowly, gathering anthers.

"You shot the pool, Henry," he said.

"It's my fault. I shouldn't have jumped around so much."

Gil was sanguine. "Don't blame yourself. Maybe the pool had it
coming."

Papa squatted down with a groan and began to snatch up the
ammunition wrappers littered on the ground. "Never you mind him,
George, never you mind him at all. He's just a contrary old man. You
can find one most anywhere. They like to sit off to the side, and
criticize, and pick, and pester, and make a general nuisance of
themselves.

"Back when I was organizing, we had a name for them: we called
them Company Grannies, because when there was an action, all they
did was stay at home, complaining and clutching their skirts, and
when we finally got the bosses to the table, finally got them to sign
the contract and give us our share, the Company Grannies would tell
us that we should have made a better deal."

He hauled himself up and held on to the shooting tripod while he
caught his breath.

It was from my grandfather that I came by my new height and
gangly frame, but while he still maintained a couple of inches on me
his spine had developed a pronounced hook, which locked him into
the permanent stoop of a man who has been kicked in the shin. Papa
hung over me with his rheumy brown eyes, batting them against the
late light in a way that was almost girlish. My mother believed that
losing Nana had broken his heart and scooped him out.

My mother didn't know about the sniper's nest we were assem-
bling in the guest room.

"Of course, I've come to realize that this particular sobriquet was a
grave slander against elderly females, most of whom can at least be
counted on to make a fine dessert now and then, and who were at one
time a useful part of society, but there you are.

"In any event, although this particular specimen will be dead soon, as you get older you should be prepared to a meet a great many more like him."

"That's true enough," said Gil. He held the roach clip up to the light, and daintily picked away a few tiny embers. "But I will guarantee you of one thing: Al Gore, the very man himself, would not approve."

"Do you want to shoot at me some more tomorrow?" I interjected this question hopefully.

Papa patted me on the shoulder. "Don't worry, George. You did your best. You did your part. I just needed to get a feel for the weapon. You just keep doing your part, help keep this old man on his toes, and everything will work out fine."

He gazed off across the paint-spattered lawn, and a thoughtful smile played across his face, as if he were seeing across a great distance to a beautiful vista that was invisible to us. "When the time comes, I'll plug the little son-of-a-bitch."

We dismantled the tripod and packed the rifle and the ammunition to take upstairs.

He ordered Gil to make himself useful and go around the front and stand by the sign to give us some perspective. "And roll up another one of those," he said, making a smoking gesture.

Then, when we were just inside, Papa stopped and turned back. He threw the sliding door open and stuck out his head to say one last thing: "And you leave Al Gore out of this, goddammit. He's suffered enough."

2.

In the guest room I remounted the rifle behind the small window that overlooked the front yard. Through the scope I sighted on Gil. Hunched over his walker, he was blithely rolling a spliff on the hood of my grandfather's Buick. A few feet away on the grass, the 15 × 15-foot sign was positioned at an angle to the street, to confront the drivers who drove north up Dundee Avenue, heading toward the South Portland mall and the I-95 ramp. From the back, the sign was a plain wall of pale blue plastic, but earlier, while I scrubbed off the spray paint, I memorized the contents of the opposite side, which were printed in large bold letters, stark and undeniable:

> Albert Gore Jr. won the 2000 election by 537,179 votes, but lost the presidency by 1 vote. DISGRACE. The leader of the free world is now a man who went AWOL from his National Guard unit, a huckster of fraudulent securities, a white-knuckle alcoholic, and a gleeful executor of the mentally handicapped. CRIMINAL. Our nation is in the midst of a coup d'état, perpetrated by a right-wing cadre that destroys the environment in the name of prosperity, hoards in the name of fairness, intimidates the voices of its critics in the name of patriotism, and wraps itself in the word of God. FARCE.

And below that there was a solemn ink portrait of Gore, underscored by the legend:

THE REAL PRESIDENT OF THE UNITED STATES.

I drew the curtain and tucked it over the rifle. The end of the barrel still poked from the corner of the open window, but in the shadow of the eaves it would be invisible from the outside, even if someone were looking.

The effort of carrying all of the gear upstairs had exhausted Papa. He collapsed into a straight-backed chair in the corner of the room and watched in silence as I reassembled the gun. There was a jar of peanuts on the side table. He uncapped it and fished around with one finger. He spoke without looking up. "Well, that should just about do it, I think. Yes, sir, indeed. That should do it. Your grandfather is now a full-fledged lunatic."

"What's that make me?" I asked.

"My henchman," he said. "How's Gilbert coming along?"

I bent down and looked through the Illustrator's scope. Gil was still picking through his battered peppermint tin of buds. "He's working on it."

Papa sighed. In the blue gloom, his face was tired and sunken. He crunched a peanut.

This was the room where, a few months earlier, my grandmother had lain in hospice.

A series of mostly black-and-white 5 × 9 photographs in plain frames crossed the walls in a band: Martin Luther King Jr., FDR, JFK, Walter Reuther, Mother Jones, Cesar Chavez, Joseph Hill-strom, and others, all of them dead, most of them martyred. During one visit my mother described the decorating motif as "Vintage Progressive." Emma wondered out loud if they might do something to brighten up the place. To this Papa replied very smartly that as far as he was concerned, the room couldn't be much brighter: the walls were "covered with stars." Unable to speak, Nana signaled her concordance with this declaration by raising one small wrinkled fist, like the black sprinters in the 1968 Olympics. To this, my parent threw up her hands. If I ever wondered why she got pregnant at eighteen, Emma said, there was all the answer I needed.

It was a few weeks later that I trotted upstairs with the newspaper to read my grandmother the latest travesty—the Bush Administration had pulled the country from the Kyoto Protocol—and discovered her staring at the photograph of Joseph Hillstrom, with that expression of recoil frozen on her face, as if Nana's last living act had been to take a sip of curdled milk.

Now, it was July, the summer of 2001, and my grandfather was alone, save for the company of his discontent, which was ample. I understood; I had problems of my own.

In the framed photograph above Papa's head, even Woody Guthrie seemed to have an idea of the direction things were heading. Woody was seated on a guitar case, his clothes white with dust, his jaw spattered with a sickly growth of beard and a ragged straw hat perched way back on his crown. On his face Woody wore the resigned grin of a man expecting to be punched and eager just to get it over with.

"Well? What do you think? Have I lost it?" Papa rubbed a palm over his twitching eye and blinked at the floor.

I examined my fingernails. "No," I said.

He glanced up, cock-eyed, still twitching.

"Maybe," I said.

"I don't know either, George." He pushed himself to his feet and his knees went through a series of rhythmic cracks, like a figure on the castanets. "But what about him, though—do you think he's crazy?"

Of course, by *him*, Papa meant Steven Sugar, his ex-Sunday paperboy, who I knew better as the commander of my high school's two-soldier chapter of the ROTC. The history of their dispute dated back to June, when my grandfather's Sunday *New York Times* began to arrive without the Travel section.

When Papa called to point out this discrepancy, the paperboy immediately barked that he would come over to discuss the problem "face to face, sir." Roughly ten minutes later Steven Sugar appeared on my grandfather's porch and dispensed a half-dozen severe cracks with the decorative brass knocker before Papa could get the door open.

A big round boy with a black brush cut and full freckled cheeks, Steven Sugar had a cuddly quality that was in no way offset by his full camouflage uniform. He listened to Papa's complaint at ramrod attention, his slight paunch jutting forward, jaw tipped up. In spite of this posture, however, my grandfather later said that he detected a smirking certainty about the boy, a glimmer of amusement in his eyes. It was a glimmer that my grandfather associated with petty-minded civil servants—state troopers, town selectman, postal clerks.

"I can assure you that I check each and every copy thoroughly, Mr. McGlaughlin," said Steven Sugar.

"Nonetheless," said the retired president of Local 219 to the ROTC Captain of Amberson County–Joshua Chamberlain Academy, "My Sunday *New York Times* lacks a Travel section."

"You must have lost it, sir," said Steven Sugar, then added helpfully, "old people lose things all the time."

This exchange instigated Papa's first complaint against the delivery service. In July, when the Style section started to disappear, too, and the Travel section had still failed to be reinserted, he lodged a second complaint. It was this protest which led, summarily, to the decision of the delivery service to remove Steven Sugar from his route; and then, to that now *ex*-paperboy's reappearance on Henry McGlaughlin's porch.

"Listen here, young man," said Papa, yanking the door open before Steven Sugar could slam the knocker again. "Your service was unsatisfactory. I voiced my dissatisfaction. You have apparently been fired. This was not my intention. My intention was to receive the entire Sunday *New York Times*, which I paid for. This is where my involvement in the matter ends. Your employment is wholly beyond my sphere of responsibility."

Steven Sugar's large face reddened.

Seeing how upset the boy was, Papa tried to soften the blow with some advice. "Well, do you have tenure? If there's some sort of tenure system for paperboys, then you might have some recourse."

"Recourse? Recourse?" The paperboy pulled off his camouflage hat and slapped it against his thigh.

At the bottom of the steps, his lieutenant, the only other member of our high school's ROTC, stood with their bicycles. A lanky, frail boy named Tolson—who, like me, would be a sophomore at Joshua Chamberlain Academy in the fall, while Sugar would be a senior—glared and squeezed the brake handles.

"Yes, recourse. That is, some means of appealing your termination."

"Fuck you," Steven Sugar told my grandfather, and flipped him off with both fingers. "You can go fuck yourself right in the ass with your recourse."

The paperboy climbed onto his bicycle and, with his lieutenant, made a couple of circles on the lawn, both of them flying double birds. Then they took off, Tolson ripping a divot with his back wheel, and Steven Sugar howling, "This isn't over, you shitheel!"

That was the part everyone laughed about. "Shitheel," said Gil, clearly delighted. "That's one I haven't heard in a while."

"It's old school," I said.

Gil cackled, waving smoke.

"Hey, Old School." My grandfather snapped his fingers for the bowl they were sharing. "Pass that along."

It happened that this incident nearly coincided with the delivery of my grandfather's billboard. He had composed the text some time after Nana died, and ordered it professionally made by a union printer in Providence.

"Take a good long look, George," Papa said to me when I came over to see the sign. He wore a big smile on his face as he tapped the text with a finger. "This is what democracy looks like." He moved his finger to the drawing of Al Gore. "And this: this is what a president looks like."

The first attack took place a week after that. Spray-painted across Al Gore's face, in glaring pink, the words: **GET OVER IT SHITHEEL! YOU LOST!**

From the get-go, there was only one suspect. "Get over it? Get over it?" my grandfather asked rhetorically, as the two of us rubbed at the paint with soapy sponges. "Who does this little terrorist think he is, George Will?"

Then, no sooner had the sign been cleaned than it was vandalized for a second time, and on this occasion Papa had stumbled out of bed to investigate a clatter outside. They were gone before he could make a positive identification, but down the street, he thought he saw a pair of diminishing forms on bicycles. There were also two other pieces of evidence: first, a second act of vandalism against the billboard—**LOVE IT OR LEAVE IT SHITHEEL!**—and perhaps more ominously, a hunter's flare that he discovered still smoldering in the hedge alongside the house.

Papa stomped out the flare, then went inside and called Gil. They had watched satellite television and smoked buds until first light, at which time Henry McGlaughlin went into action.

Summarily, he placed phone calls to Mr. and Mrs. Rodney Sugar of 113 Elkington Drive, then to the Amberson Township Police, and, finally, for good measure, the ACLU.

Papa offered no introduction to the Sugars, but went right to the crux: "Your son has impinged on my free speech, and I want to know what you plan to do about it."

"Pardon?" asked the groggy female voice on the other end of the line.

"My free speech has been impinged. Violated. Trod upon. My First Amendment right. By your son."

There was a moment of silence before Mrs. Sugar gathered her wits. "Free speech? At five-twenty in the morning? Are you serious? Well shit on you, you crazy old coot."

She hung up, but before lunch the Sugars' lawyer messengered over a response. *Mr. McGlaughlin*, the attorney wrote, *we are aware of, and sympathetic to, your recent loss . . . However, if this harassment continues, on behalf of my clients we are prepared to apply for a restraining order . . .*

The investigating police sergeant gave the area around the sign a cursory inspection, and grimly scratched his goatee with his un-opened notebook. "Okay, chief," said the officer, "It does appear that we have a case of vandalism on our hands."

"Yes, my former paperboy—"

"I know, I know. But there's no proof. The parents say you've got the wrong man, and you're ready for the bughouse to boot. Now, that's not for me to say, but"—the officer paused, and made a point of sniffing the air—"are you aware that cannabis is illegal in the state of Maine, Mr. McGlaughlin?"

My grandfather took a deep breath and looked up at the sky. "Are you aware, Officer Corcoran, of a document called the United States Constitution? It has a list of amendments—laws, that is—the first of which gives me the right to free speech."

The officer flipped his notebook open, squinted at a blank page, and flipped the notebook shut again. "If that's how you want to play it, chief, that's fine with me." He put his hands on his hips and shook his head at the ground. He licked the mustache of his goatee with the tip of his tongue. "Let's face it, a sign like this, I bet it pisses a lot of people off.

"Tell you the truth, it kind of pisses me off. It's unpatriotic as hell if you ask me. Now look, I believe in free speech as much as the next guy, but not so far as this sort of garbage goes. What do you think about that, chief?"

"I think," said Papa, "that you have a very nice goatee, Officer."

The ACLU lawyer came third. Papa told her the whole story, and she listened, asking a few questions, but mostly staying quiet. When he finished, she apologized. "There's no angle, Mr. M."

"What about my free speech? How's that for an angle? You know, I gave money to you jokers when it meant something. I gave when Hoover was in office."

"Your free speech isn't being violated by an entity here, sir, just by a paperboy. Look, if your paperboy were being funded by an interest group, or backed by the KKK or something, I'd have this thing on the front page of *USA Today* tomorrow." Papa heard the hiss of compressed air as the ACLU lawyer opened a soda. "Besides, and I'm hardly being facetious here, but down in D.C. we've got Ashcroft probably planning to compile a database of everyone who's ever had fun before. If we let this guy out of our sight for a minute, he'll start having people scourged for picking their wedge on the Sabbath. Really, sir, and with all due respect to the good and honorable work you've done, when it comes to brass balls, Old Mary Hoover couldn't have budged the pair that Ashcroft is hauling around. Take my word, as an American citizen in the year 2001, a dink paperboy is not the worst problem you've got."

Of course, by this time, my grandfather's Sunday *New York Times* had become something else entirely. Which brought us up to the present day, and the third attack, the one that had convinced my grandfather to settle matters himself.

I could not recall ever having spoken to Steven Sugar, or even having heard his voice, although he was a familiar sight in the halls: a chunky kid two grades ahead of me, who clomped from class to class in his combat boots and baggy desert-toned fatigues, usually followed a few steps behind by the lieutenant, Tolson.

Still, before all of this—before **GET OVER IT SHITHEEL! YOU LOST!**

before **LOVE IT OR LEAVE IT SHITHEEL!** and, before **COMMUNIST SHITHEEL!** were scarred in blazing pink across my grandfather's billboard and Al Gore's face—I didn't know if I ever spared Steven Sugar so much as a single conscious thought.

Now I imagined him punching through the dark suburbs on his bicycle, the summer night rushing through his brush cut, the newspaper satchel packed with spray cans clattering against his hip, a vessel of absolute calm and purpose, locked and loaded, a true believer and an armed combatant. The vision amazed me, and a part of me envied him, this budding fascist who had fucked up my grandfather's Sunday *New York Times* and written right across his First Amendment rights. I could only marvel at his confidence, at his criminal's justification. I did not understand Steven Sugar's motives, but I sensed his satisfaction, like a dark mass on a radar screen, like an iceberg, and grand like an iceberg, too.

I pictured Steven Sugar, hunched under the tent of his blankets, as he crinkled through the purloined newspapers by flashlight. He turned over the last unsullied islands of the Mediterranean, the white beaches and the ancient piles of stone, and he licked his lips over column inches of the weddings of well-to-do young women in Manhattan, with Ivy League degrees and careers in handbag design.

What did it mean to him? Did he imagine laying waste to these beautiful landscapes, and rolling tanks through rustic villages? Did he fantasize of ripping these bright new wives from their honeymoons and their husbands? Or, maybe, he hated our little Maine town, and longed more than anything just to travel far away, to start again, and make his life in another country altogether. Was it possible that Steven Sugar read the wedding announcements for research, for that time ten years from now when he would be a surgeon (or a hedge fund tycoon), and it would be time to marry his own twenty-six-year-old producer of a children's television show (or director of marketing at a glossy magazine), his own pretty, pale-eyed Hannah (or Caroline)? Maybe it didn't mean anything to him. Maybe Steven Sugar stole from my grandfather's newspaper for the simplest reason—just because he could.

Just because he could. The idea raised the skin on my forearms and caused me to breathe through my mouth.

My grandfather placed an expectant hand on my shoulder, and repeated his question. "Well, what is it? What do you really think, George? Is he crazy, or he is angry?"

"No," I said. "I don't think Steven Sugar's crazy. I think he's just angry."

Papa squeezed my shoulder and walked across the room to the window. "Then that makes us even, because I may be crazy, but I surely am angry, too." The old man bent over the rifle and peered into the scope. "And I've come to realize that the only way to talk to these monsters is to speak in a language they understand."

3.

The difficulty of communication was, in fact, the source of my own personal distress. I wasn't getting along with my mother, and I didn't care to get along with Dr. Vic. Of late, I suffered not so much from a feeling that my voice wasn't being heard, as from a sense that I was speaking an entirely different language. Or perhaps, I thought, to their ears my voice was soundless, on the wrong frequency, like a dog whistle, and they only waited for the moment that my lips stopped moving to smile, and shake their heads, and explain what it was that I failed to understand.

We had moved into Dr. Vic's place that winter, a sprawling new three-story that sat right on the shore of Lake Keynes. From the window of my attic loft I had an obstructed panorama of the lake, which spanned a couple of miles across, toward pine-covered foot-hills and farther away, to a bald mountainside where tourists came to ski in December. This vantage point also offered a clear view of the deck, and the landing where Dr. Vic tied up his putt-putt and his kayak.

Earlier that summer they were engaged, and since the weather warmed up, my mother and her lover had kept a nightly ritual of

dancing on the landing at the end of the deck. They took a portable stereo out with them, along with a stack of CDs, a couple of mugs, and a can of insect repellant, and sometimes stayed for hours, slow dancing until the early morning. Their object was to find their "wedding song," the perfect song for their first dance as a married couple.

The sounds of Dr. Vic's music collection drifted up in a tinny echo, and if I wanted I could watch them from my window. Instead, I sat beneath the sill, back against the wall, and hated myself for even wondering what song they would pick, for surreptitiously playing along with their stupid game. Between songs I caught snatches of their conversations, their laughter, the clink of their toasts.

Frequently, Dr. Vic's taste sent my mother into paroxysms of laughter, and I would hear her rolling around on the deck, overcome by it, as if he were the funniest guy in the world. The sound dropped through me like a heavy object released from a great height, and never seemed to hit bottom.

One night I heard her scream with delight at the discovery of a Don Johnson CD. It was like finding his porn stash, she whooped. My mother laughed and beat her bare feet on the deck.

"Come on," said Dr. Vic. "You liked him, too, you know you did. You know you never missed an episode."

This was porn, she howled, this was emotional porn. *Crockett Sings Just for You*! My mother began to weep as she laughed.

"Wait a second, wait a second. 'Heartbeat' is good. Seriously, you've got to admit that 'Heartbeat' is a pretty good song." Now Dr. Vic was snickering, too.

A few moments passed before my mother could speak again. She thought she'd fallen for a respectable country doctor, Emma gasped, but in actuality, she had fallen for a nine-year-old girl from 1984, and oh, my God, was it wrong that she loved him anyway? Because she did. She loved him, loved him, loved him.

Their kisses were inaudible, but I was old enough to know that was what came next. Sometimes they listened to CDs until the night turned gray, and after I fell asleep Dr. Vic's middle-aged music, the Wynton Marsalis and the Phil Collins and the terrible seventies pop which all seemed to bear edible names—Bread and Juice Newton and Humble Pie—infiltrated my subconscious and provided the soundtrack for my dreams. I chased after them in these dreams, my mother and her fiancé, as they strolled arm in arm along crowded sidewalks and through parks and malls. I ran beside them and jumped around and screamed for my mother to listen to me, to fucking turn that shit off and listen to me, because I had something to say, something very important to say. At most, Dr. Vic might shush me, or my mother might give him a look of apology, but they never stopped, and in the morning there were tears of frustration crusted beneath my eyes. I was embarrassed by the childish obviousness of these dreams, and the way that I could feel them gathering inside of me even when I was awake, each angry observation floating up like a little black balloon, until night came again and my sky jostled with them.

It seemed that I was letting go of those balloon strings all day long: every time I saw him rub her shoulders while she sat reading a book; every time I saw her standing outside with him in a cold drizzle, holding the umbrella while he walked his dogs; every time we drove somewhere and Dr. Vic told me to go ahead and take the front, and I knew that it was something that they discussed in private and decided to give me.

To them, I was just the jealous kid of a single mother, with no understanding of sex or intimacy, or the difference between a lover's love and a child's love, and why an adult needed both. To me, this was a slanderous lie. Dr. Vic was the exception. We had lived all over and my mother had dated all sorts of different men, and there was never a problem before.

In Blue Hill, there had been Paul, the raccoon-eyed owner of a pottery studio for tourists, who helped me fire and paint a cookie jar in the shape of a Jerry Bear for Emma's birthday. When my mother worked at the University of Maine, she dated a German graduate student named Jupps, who would let me watch anything I wanted on television, and laugh uproariously, no matter if the show was about ski slope accidents, or the big bang. The first year we moved home to Yarmouth, before Nana got sick and before my mother took the job at the local branch of Planned Parenthood and met Dr. Vic, she went out with Dale, the editor of the local weekly, the *Amberson Common*. Dale and I used to play a game where I tried to guess the classifieds that he made up, things like,

Wanted:
SWM seeks cheeseburger, Coke, respect

CAN YOU PITCH?
Lefthander wntd. Must be bipedal, animate. Respondents should report immed to Fenway Park, Boston, MA.

After they broke up, Dale posted me a classified that said,

Old White Dude:
OWD can provide referncs, illeg firewrks, home remdies, etc. Cool kid always welc.

I liked them all—even Jupps, who reeked of mouthwash and sometimes unnerved me with his maniacal laughter. That was because these men simply accepted my presence, and let me determine the level of our interaction. They had, so to speak, paid their dues.

The evening after my grandfather used me for target practice, I offered to take Dr. Vic's two yapping little Pekinese—"the Laddies," he insisted on calling them—for a walk while dinner was on the patio grill. This was something I had been doing a lot lately, to Dr. Vic's obvious pleasure. "Even after the longest winter, there is a thaw," I overheard him whisper to my mother.

But my mother knew me better. Now, sitting nearby on a lawn chair, she indicated her suspicion with a deep breath.

"Don't put up with any guff from those rascals, okay?" said my mother's fiancé. He chuckled and sipped his glass of white wine. His clip-on sunglasses were slightly askew.

"Nice shades, Doc," I said.

"Thank ya very much," he said, like Elvis.

I turned from him to sneer at my mother. She shrugged, tapped her finger against the zipper of her shorts. I rolled my eyes at her. She tapped the zipper of her shorts again. I looked downward—then jerked up my fly and started into the house.

"You know, Emma, I think that our young George here, may just have stumbled upon one of the great secrets of manhood here," said Dr. Vic, and I didn't have to see the huge, open-faced smile that he was giving to my mother to know it was there. "Back in my single days, I took the Laddies from pillar to post and back again. It might seem a little devious, but a regular guy has to make his breaks where he can, and not everybody can play guitar. For a regular guy, a dog is the next best thing to being a musician. You might even say that the Laddies are 'The Bomb.'" He emphasized this statement with index finger quotation marks. "You might even say that they're 'The Shit.'"

This was typical of Dr. Vic, to make a big, cheesy production out of everything, even the names of his dogs. Every time he spoke, his wide doughy face opening up in a way that reminded me of the singing clams in Disney's *Alice in Wonderland*, I felt a little part of myself die from shame. In fact, I believed that Dr. Vic must be the most embarrassing person in the world.

To begin with, there were the little absurdist poems that he wrote about how much he loved my mother, and what he would do if she were suddenly transformed into something other than herself, something inanimate usually, like a toaster or a grape—

The Woman I Love Is A Grape (For The Purposes Of This Poem)
By Victor Lipscomb
If she were a grape and I was still an ape
I'd wait for days and try to think of some way
Not to eat her, to reanimate her
But if I had to, I'd be glad to

Because Emma is so sweet.

For our enjoyment, he taped these poems to the fridge, like a first-grader would his watercolors.

Then there was his music, of course, the awful songs Dr. Vic always listened to in his car and in his study, stuff like "Seasons in the Sun" and "Dreamweaver"; songs that were so damned impossible to stop singing to yourself they were like dippy little Post-it Notes pasted to the inside of your skull, and until the glue dried up and the note fell off, there was nothing you could do to defend yourself against the insipid, endless trickling of the Dreamweaver's synthesizer, or to keep from chanting, helplessly, over and over again, "We had joy, we had fun, we had seasons in the sun."

And Dr. Vic talked to his crossword puzzles; every time he found the answer "Yoko," or "Ono," he cried out, "There she is again!" like he was in a bingo parlor; and when he poured wine for my mother, he stood with a dish towel over his wrist and twirled the end of an invisible mustache while he waited for her to nod; and in restaurants, Dr. Vic liked to hand his credit card to the cashier and make an introduction, "Peter: Paul, Paul: Peter"; and finally—and I thought, most tellingly of all—there were the utility pants he wore, which drooped from the weight of all the hard candies and dog treats that he stuffed in the tiny pockets, so that much of the time he walked around with one hand holding up his belt, like a goddamned clown.

There was a horrifying optimism in everything he did, which struck me as completely false, even as I knew that he could not be more sincere—that he was, really, incapable of insincerity. Everything about him—his clomping steps, his bright, solid-colored L.L. Bean shirts, the deflated tube of a belly that hung over his belt—testified to this irrefutable fact.

Dr. Vic could be wounded, but he could not be discouraged. When he told me that all of this was "a life passage," I could see in his eyes that he was actually imagining some abstract tunnel in his own mind, with a bright light at the end, and the sound of chirping birds and jingling ice cream trucks.

Perhaps there was nothing more at the heart of my dislike for my mother's fiancé than simple incredulity. I was the son of a single mother. I had lived in neighborhoods where ice cream trucks didn't go. It seemed to me that good will could only carry a person so far, and after that, you were on your own.

How this tenet translated into my current sabotage campaign was not completely clear even to me, but I knew this was not the time for hesitation, or half measures.

In the pantry freezer I retrieved the small plastic bag hidden under a mound of ice behind a stack of swordfish steaks. I slipped on an oven mitt and herded the Laddies into the front yard and down to the meadow that lay a few hundred yards west of the house. Well trained by weeks of practice, the two Pekinese bolted forward in full play mode. They dashed ahead and then dashed back to implore me to hurry up. Their entire hind ends wagged with enthusiasm.

"Okay, okay," I said, and pulled one of the frozen turds out of the bag and hurled it across the field. The Laddies tore after the soaring brown lump, disappearing in a wake of trembling blue bonnets.

The notion that there was anything cruel about teaching my prospective stepfather's dogs to fetch their own feces, or that there was something more than a little demented about the trouble that I had gone to—sneaking outside after dark to pick up these pieces of crap and then freezing them so that they could be thrown—did occur to me at a few odd moments. Luckily, I was usually able to slough off such attacks of conscience. If this was a war—and it was—would a real soldier—like Steven Sugar—be able to worry about a couple of crap-eating toy dogs who weren't even smart enough to have their own names? Somewhere along the line, probably in a Vietnam movie, I had picked up the term "collateral damage," and it seemed to apply quite nicely to the situation at hand.

I even had a line I wanted to use on Dr. Vic, and I imagined myself saying it like Gil, with a wink and a smirk, punctuated by a big, jolly armpit fart. "Seems to me that there's nothing worse than a shit-eating dog," I would wryly observe, and then wait a moment before adding, "except maybe two shit-eating dogs."

After a few tosses the frozen turds inevitably began to soften, and I quickly worked through the bag, chucking the shit into the high grass until my shoulder started to click. The dogs were relentless, though, tumbling off in pursuit and returning with wild foaming grins, the hard black biscuits clamped in their jaws.

Somewhere around the twentieth throw, one of them limped back, dropped a turd, and collapsed at my feet. The dog gave a few strangled retches and panted heavily. Its eyes slid anxiously back and forth; the dog coughed, and seemed to pant harder.

Sensing his brother's weakness, the other Laddie darted in and snatched up the crap, then bolted into the grass to hoard his prize.

The sick Pekinese flopped onto its side. I knelt down, feeling my stomach give a twist. "Shit poisoning," I thought to myself, unsure if such a condition even existed.

I laid a hand on the animal's flank, and he lurched up. He looked up from beneath his mop tassel bangs and grinned. The dog licked my palm. I let him for a moment before realizing where his tongue had been. I slapped his snout. The dog jerked away and yipped in protest.

"Jesus, okay," I said. "Okay, I'm sorry."

Leading them inside, I reminded the dogs that I didn't feel sorry for them. "You don't even know any better," I said.

My mother watched me grab a handful of dog bones from the cookie jar. The Laddies started crunching happily. She blew a strand of dark hair from her eye and nodded questioningly at the oven mitt still on my hand. I shrugged and crumpled it back in its drawer.

I'm thirty-three years old and I can damn well do what I please, my mother wrote.

As a form of nonviolent protest I had stopped speaking to her. Not deigning to explain the nature of my demonstration, or even that it was a demonstration, I simply started carrying around a yellow legal pad for those occasions when communication was unavoidable. Maddeningly, my mother had responded by refusing to speak to me as well, and purchased her own yellow legal pad. Now, instead of yelling at each other, we argued by shoving our legal pads back and forth across Dr. Vic's dinner table.

This particular argument started with the oven mitt. What had I been doing with it, my mother wanted to know, and why did it smell

so funny? My evasions quickly led to the inevitable destination of all
our arguments these days, to the real heart of the matter. That is:
Why are you doing this to me? Have you looked at the man sitting
across the table? That foolish-looking man over there? The roly-poly
one with the American flag tie thrown over his shoulder? You're
going to marry him? That guy? Him?

How can you be so stupid? How could anyone be so stupid?

*I've done a lot of stupid things in my life, George Claiborne, not
the least of which was giving birth to a child at the age of nineteen.
However, that particular error in judgment has turned out to be the
greatest joy of my life, in spite of your current behavior. A lot of
people called me stupid when I kept you. Stupid and I have a pretty
fair track record.*

I knew I was vulnerable on the matter of my conception, so I
responded by jotting down a favorite stanza from one of Dr. Vic's
poems:

> *If she were a toaster, I'd make a toaster-coaster*
> *If she were a toaster, I'd be a toaster-boaster*

As she wrote, my mother pressed down so hard the pen made a
whining sound. *What does any of this have to do with him? He's
never done a thing to you. Although it would be hard to blame him if
he did.*

I hated the way she underlined things. *You're a blackleg.*

*You're a little shit, and furthermore, you don't have the first idea
what that word means. You're just reaching for the nearest pejora-
tive, George. This isn't the legend of one of your grandfather's
strikes. This is the story of a little boy who still has a hell of a lot
of growing up to do.*

At the end of the table Dr. Vic sawed morosely at a chicken breast.
He dabbed at his damp face with his patriotic tie. "I feel like I should
get a notebook," he said, but no one answered.

While she awaited a response, my mother maintained a posture of
nunlike serenity, hands folded, long black hair tucked neatly behind
her ears. Her first streak of gray had appeared that spring; a fine,

silvery tributary of her part that I hoped was a biological reaction to her agonized conscience, although to this stage she had conceded nothing. A few mornings, in the bathrooms of those crummy apartments in Orono and Blue Hill and Waterville, after a night of drinking with her friends or her lover, I held that hair back while she vomited.

My grandparents had taught me about sides, about the line that separated one side from the other side, and the impossibility of straddling that line. You were either in, or you were out. Until Dr. Vic came along, the men in my mother's life had always gone about trying to get on *our* side. But when it came to Dr. Vic, my mother told me that some things were not open to negotiation. All the years of moving from one town to another while she made her hiccuping way toward a bachelor's degree, all the years of crummy apartments with three fuzzy channels and hose showers and cat hair in the corners, all of it had been an alliance of convenience. Now I saw that the two of them, Emma and Dr. Vic, were on their own side, and I was on the other, and there was a very real line separating us. Now she looked at me like that, with her hands clasped and her back straight, like a study hall proctor.

". . . And I've come to realize that the only way to talk to these monsters is to speak in a language they understand." That was the way Papa had put it.

I wanted to throw gravy in her face.

He let Nana die, I wrote and sent my notebook skidding across the table.

Later that night, she knocked on my door, and when I opened it, just stood there. Her cheeks were stained with tear tracks, and her eyes seemed to be directed at a point somewhere over my shoulder.

"Well?" I asked.

Her hand flew up, and I heard the report of the slap before I felt it. The sound seemed to expand, to fill the entire house, to carry across the lake and into the wooded hills, like a gunshot. I didn't even take a step back; I was too startled.

My mother's expression never changed. Her gaze still focused on that place behind me. Emma reached into her pocket and threw a balled up note rattling across the floor. Very softly, she closed the door.

When I was alone the memory of her tear streaks gave me solace, even as I forced myself to cry a little. The note said, *Someday, you will be ashamed of the way you acted tonight.*

I was further comforted by the slamming of doors downstairs, and the echoes of my mother yelling, and of her lover—my late grandmother's oncologist and my prospective stepfather, Victor Lipscomb, M.D., Ph.D.—trying to calm her. His deep voice pleaded up through the heating vents: "Emma, honey," and, "Come on," and, "We just have to keep working at this." Nor was I unhappy to register, as I drifted to sleep, the quiet of a night without music.

I awoke from a nightmare at dawn, gasping and rubbing the sheets against my chest, attempting to wipe off the words that Steven Sugar had spray-painted on my body.

In the nightmare I was tied to a tree, and the Richard Nixon mask was on my face, making it hard to breathe. From the shadows, a figure emerged; Steven Sugar was dressed in his army fatigues and his eyes were my mother's eyes, dark and unforgiving. He held a spray can.

As I wriggled and cried for help, he patiently filled in the letters, bending the words around my torso in cheap red paint. **GET OVER IT SHITHEEL! YOU LOST!**

4.

Stationed in the guest room, my grandfather and I kept watch through the next afternoon, and waited for Steven Sugar to make his move. The lights were off to keep the room cool, and the main source of illumination came from outside, through the curtains. The filtered light spilled across the room in a bright orange column. Papa sat in the chair alongside the rifle and tripod, and flicked back the curtain every minute or so to see if anything was moving on the C-curve segment of the street that was visible from the window.

For the most part, we sat in silence. I had simply showed up and plopped down on the guest room bed. Papa said, "Howdy," without glancing from his window. In the attic I had discovered a box of my mother's brittle old Choose Your Own Adventure paperbacks—where you moved through the story according to your own strategic decisions—and I absently paged through one entitled *The Alien's Tomb*. Out of the corner of my eye, I kept an eye on Papa; light fell across his forehead, and made him look young. I wondered if he was thinking about my grandmother.

If you trust the dead alien, and follow him through the doorway into the Forever Country, turn to page 12. If you retrace your footsteps to the nearest Time Pod, turn to page 34.

"You should be out with your friends." He lifted the corner of the curtain, grimaced at the street, and dropped it back down.

"I haven't got any," I said. "Not really."

He sucked on a peanut, then slowly ground it up. "I hold this claim in dubious regard."

"We moved too much." My mother and I had lived in six towns so far during my school-age years, which in adolescent terms made me a kind of Okie. It wasn't that I didn't get along with people, or nod to friendly acquaintances in the halls at school. Rather, I thought, very rationally, that growing up was embarrassing enough without trying to gain an invitation to the party. Maybe I was more lonely than I let on; maybe after two years in the Amberson school system it was time to accept that my boyhood fantasy of staying put in one place had finally become a reality. Then again, I found it hard to accept Dr. Vic as a part of any dream come true.

If you stay with the jackass and his shit-snarfing dogs, turn to page 11. If you ramble on to another town, turn to page 45.

"A boy ought to have friends, George."

"I'm fifteen."

"Pardon me. A teenager ought to have friends, George."

"I get along with people."

"Well," he said.

"Well," I said.

He pulled back the curtain, looked, let go of it. My grandfather cast a sideward glance in my direction. I raised my eyebrows at him and brushed at the collar of my T-shirt. He snorted, flicked the peanut crumbs from his button-down.

"You're afraid, aren't you? It's a risk, isn't it? To try and break the ice?"

"Sure." I wasn't about to deny it.

Papa rocked back and patted his knees and nodded, as if that just about made everything obvious. "Well, you're a goddamned freak, aren't you?"

This statement hung in the air between us for a minute. My grandfather stared at me with perfect assurance; I was too baffled to be hurt.

"Thanks a lot," I said, finally. "That helps. That really helps a lot."

"I mean, kids are curious. They love freaks."

"Jesus, Papa. This is great. Do you think you might be able to give me a kick in the nuts, too?"

"No, no," he said, and drew his foot up over his knee. He patted his slipper. "Your toe. Show your toe. It's a conversation starter. It's interesting."

I slumped back on the bed.

"Let me see it," he said. "Come on."

"See this," I said, and showed him my middle finger.

The old man cackled, then turned his attention to the watch.

So, I read the rest of *The Alien's Tomb,* and following a series of wrong turns and misadventures, discovered that the best I could do was to get back to the place where I had started.

At some point, I nodded off, and woke up to see Joseph Hillstrom staring back at me. The man in the black-and-white photograph was hatchet-faced, and his eyes held a spooky clarity, almost like a blind man's eyes. It was a gaze that seemed not so much to look into the camera, as beyond the camera. I rolled away from him.

Beside the window, Papa was still in his chair, and slightly slumped, so that now the sunlight fell on his hair, and revealed the pink scalp beneath.

I turned onto my back and blinked at the ceiling, letting myself come all the way up.

It was Nana who had told me the story of Hillstrom, the song-writer and organizer, convicted on circumstantial evidence and executed in Utah in 1915 for killing two men in a robbery. My grandmother said that on the night of the killing, a witness claimed to have seen Joe throw a pistol far into a field, although the weapon was never recovered. Furthermore, the police knew that one of the dead men managed to fire off a shot; and when they came to see Joe, they discovered he was bedridden with a bullet wound. Joe said he was shot defending a woman, but would not reveal her name, for it was a question of honor. On the eve of his execution, Hillstrom had been lucid and fearless enough to write to a friend, *Don't Mourn! Organize!*

And he was the last thing Nana had ever seen. I could feel sweat on my forearms. I didn't know why I was suddenly uneasy. I rolled back to look at the photograph of the dead man again.

"Old Joe is a kind of saint to the Movement, Georgie," Nana had said to me, and in the next moment, crossed her eyes to break the mood of seriousness created by a story concerning murder and execution and martyrdom. I was about seven years old at the time. "Not, mind you, that the gentleman in Rome with the silly hat and the special red telephone up to God is liable to recognize him any time soon."

I forced myself to hold the eyes in the photograph, and after a moment the uneasy feeling passed. I supposed that was how a saint should look: calm and guiltless, and made of steel that no pagan bonfire could ever melt. I supposed that was what Nana had seen.

"Gore would have rolled back NAFTA."

Papa announced this apropos of nothing.

I sat up.

My grandfather still sat as before, slumped, the light falling on his white hair. He had been awake all along.

"That's Gil's new line. NAFTA this, NAFTA that." He gave the curtain an irritable snap. His good humor seemed to have passed. "And if it's not one *N* word, it's another." He cleared his throat, and made a disgusted pronouncement: "*Nader.*

"Al Gore did more for working people last night, while he slept in his bed, than Ralph Nader has done in his whole life. That old man likes to needle me, George, and he knows how to do it."

"What's NAFTA?" I asked.

"A mistake," said Papa, and seemed to fumble for something more, before settling on "A well-intentioned mistake. A flawed document of collective bargaining. A compromise. *A com-pro-mise.* Something that son-of-a-bitch Nader wouldn't know the first thing about." Papa pulled up the corner of the curtain. "I get damned weary of all the blue cars," he said.

On my evening ride back from my grandparents' house I felt a wiggle in my rear tire, and pulled over to check it—a flat. Choosing between calling Dr. Vic to pick me up, and swinging by the clinic to get a lift to the gas station from my mother, I opted for Emma. I coasted the half mile to the professional park that housed the Planned Parenthood clinic and a number of other doctors' offices.

What I hadn't anticipated, however, was that the GFAs had attacked again.

My mother was out front, working with a bottle of Goo Gone and a putty scraper to scour off a fake picture of a mauled infant that had been plastered to the glass doors. This infant appeared not so much to have been aborted as microwaved, and then dipped in red candle wax. For that matter, the infant appeared not to be an infant so much as a doll.

I braked at the curb, and she shook her head at me. Tendrils of hair stuck to her cheeks and forehead.

"You're just in time, George," said Charlie Birdsong, the clinic's head security guard, who sat on an upside down paint bucket with his shirt off, perusing an issue of *Elle Girl*. "The GFAs have been busy with their Photoshop program again, and this time they used a buttload of Krazy Glue. And that's with special emphasis on the Krazy, doc."

Echoing this sentiment, my mother sighed wearily and knocked her skull a few times against the papered glass doors.

GFA was shorthand for God's Favorite Assholes, the name my mother had awarded to the group of Evangelical Christians who maintained an isolated community in the scrubby hills north of Amberson. Every once in a while I'd see one around town, at the supermarket or Sam's Club: the female GFAs tended to be bright eyed, and almost squirrel-like in the way they would challenge your gaze and at the same time rush past you with a giant cube of generic toilet paper; the typical male GFA was more dour in his bearing, lank haired, and often outfitted in the kind of T-shirts you could buy for a dollar at gas stations, featuring air-brushed illustrations of wolves or caribou. These good Christians eked out their livelihood largely by selling buckets of fishing worms to tourists, and otherwise mostly kept to themselves.

The exception to their isolation, unfortunately, was my mother's clinic. Until recently, they had limited themselves to staging conventional—if exuberant—pickets in front of the building, blasting Christian rock music from the back of their rusted blue minivan and using a megaphone to address the pregnant women who were rushed across the parking lot in a protective wing of volunteers. "Leave your whoremaster and come unto the Lord!" one particular GFA harpy was infamous for howling as she stomped back and forth on the roof of the minivan.

Recently, however, the GFAs had apparently discovered the power of Photoshop and taken to creating enormous posters of tattered fetuses—like the one now plastered to the glass doors of the clinic— and applying them with industrial epoxy during random, late-night guerrilla attacks. Vandalism, it seemed, was on the rise all over town.

(After the first assault on Papa's billboard, my mother had pointed out that the vandalism fit the GFA's pattern. "No," said my grandfather after a moment's thought. "It's the damn paperboy. Those kooky wormdiggers are on a mission from God. They're above politics."

There was no reason to believe that the GFAs were coached by Steven Sugar—or vice versa—but if the two ever did get together, there was no telling what kind of damage they might do.)

What's NAFTA? I asked my mother. After fifteen minutes of pouring over *Elle Girl* with Charlie my mind had started to wander.

She stepped back from the glass and took the legal pad from me. *Seriously?* My mother plucked one of my shirtsleeves to dry her sweaty hands.

I yanked away, and tapped the question impatiently with my finger: *What's NAFTA?*

My mother blew a damp bang out of her eyes and checked her watch. Her face was flushed with exertion and the poster hung in tenacious ribbons from the glass. Emma shook her head. *Ask Charlie. I want to finish dealing with the slaughtered unborn here in time to get home for the news.*

"Charlie, what's NAFTA?"

A sallow-faced, affectless Native American man, Charlie was as unimposing as any armed person could possibly be; along with his habit of whiling away his time at the security gate by reading the women's magazines from the lobby, the price sticker—$241.99— was still stuck to the bottom of the butt of his pistol.

Without looking up from *Elle Girl*, Charlie said, "NAFTA. Okay. I used to work at a shoe factory. Full health benefits, eighteen-fifty an hour, vacation, and a parking space based on seniority.

"Now, some poor destitute prick in Guatemala is working in my old company's new factory for, like, a buck an hour. Meanwhile, now I work here, get accused of murder by white people, ten dollars an hour, and have to pull weekends in the bedding department at Filene's to make ends meet. Plenty of parking spaces, too, but I had to sell my car. Now I ride the bus."

"What about the union?" I asked.

Charlie spat a laugh. "What about the union? Clinton was a Democrat, wasn't he?"

I contemplated this for a few moments, as my mother's scraper made a sound like a shovel blade being dragged across a rock.

Charlie flipped a page, sighed. "I'm telling you, it really sucks to be a fat girl."

My mother dropped me at the Citgo, and I spent a couple of minutes at the air station, pumping my tire up. Through the scarred window I could see a glass cooler filled with Styrofoam tubs of GFA fishing worms. Each label was adorned with a small hand-drawn gold cross and the promise that these were FAT WORMS! NONE FATTER!

A car honked and I turned around to see Gil and Mrs. Desjardins in their Land Rover. They waved me over. I rolled my bike over to the driver's side—Gil's side—and he lowered his window.

"Afternoon, stud," said Mrs. Desjardins, leaning over and blowing a kiss.

"It's evening, Lana."

"Evening, stud." Mrs. Desjardins smiled at me. Her lipstick was a radioactive green. She was dressed in a glittering cocktail gown.

"How's it going, kid?" Gil was wearing his silky black pajamas.

"Fine," I said. "I'm kind of wrestling with this whole NAFTA thing, though."

He took this in stride. "Okay, run in the gas station, fetch me a Coke Slurpee, some Twizzlers, a jar of petroleum jelly, and some Aleve." Gil snapped a twenty-dollar bill from his pocket. "Then you can keep the change and I'll tell you all you need to know about NAFTA."

The clerk gave me a skeptical look and rang up the purchases. "How old are you, kid?" he asked. The clerk was a Goth-type in his early twenties, with rings in each of his nostrils and a fork tattooed on his Adam's apple.

"Excuse me?"

"Forget it." He shoved the things in a paper bag and told me to scram.

In the lot I passed the bag through the window to Gil and he handed it off to his wife. "Any trouble with Count Dracula in there?"

"No," I said, not wanting to get into it.

"Right, then," said Gil, "NAFTA."

I nodded.

"Between you and me?"

"Sure," I said.

"I'll just close my ears, then," said Mrs. Desjardins.

"All you need to know about NAFTA, my boy, is this: it was inevitable. Your grandfather is going to tell you that it was a compromise. I'm telling you that it was erosion." There was a merry crinkle around Gil's eyes. It occurred to me that in a few months, or a year, I would probably be looking down on his face as he lay cushioned in velvet, hands folded on his chest. "The lobbyists had been chiseling away for fifty years. The center, politically speaking, would not hold, George. Democrats, Republicans, it doesn't matter. The money needs more money."

I nodded.

"You understand?"

"Not really."

Gil chuckled, and fingered at the top button of his black pajamas. "Look, it's a shell game. The politicians said it was about 'Free Trade.' Bullshit. It was about 'Cheap Labor.' Just like every other manner of deregulation in this country, NAFTA was just another way of pumping up corporate profits under the auspices of the 'American Way.' Gore went along with it, just like all the rest of them. Every single one of them—corporate flunkies, hypocrites— with their hands out and their eyes closed. That's the System. Gore, Bush, they're both part of it, they both run on the same track. Stick a quarter in their backs, and they'll race all day.

"And, as much as Henry disparages him, it so happens that there was, in fact, only one candidate who didn't belong to the system." He winked at me. "And that was Big Ralph."

"Big Ralph," repeated Mrs. Desjardins with a little trill, "oh, dear me."

One of my earliest memories was of my grandmother setting the needle down on a scratchy Phil Ochs 78, and his guitar strumming a melody, at once flat and deep, as if he were playing at the bottom of a hole and singing up to us:

I dreamed I saw Joe Hill last night
Alive as you and me
Says I, "But Joe you're ten years dead."
"I never died," says he.
"I never died," says he.

This memory carried strong associations with the no-bake cookies she used to make and *The New Testament Bible* that we used for my reading lessons. On the title page of that thin blue book, I remembered the minuscule parenthetical that Nana added in her cramped cursive:

THE NEW COVENANT
COMMONLY CALLED
THE NEW TESTAMENT
OF OUR LORD AND SAVIOR
JESUS CHRIST (ρ-BETHLEHEM)

"It doesn't matter if you believe in God, Georgie my love," Nana said to me once as she rubbed a wet washcloth over my chocolate-stained chin. (She was the only one who could ever call me Georgie and hope to live.) "But it's imperative that you understand Jesus was a real person. It's imperative that you realize that he was exactly the sort of man that these so-called Christians today would have pilloried for being an agitator and a Communist.

"They killed him because he was a mouthy liberal."

In her final weeks, my grandmother made no last-minute conversion or requests for spiritual assistance, although once, after Dr. Vic administered a heavy dose of morphine, she commented on the tintype of Jesus on the wall, the one that was nestled between the black-and-whites of Emma Goldberg and Joseph Hillstrom. Papa had been sitting alongside the bed, holding her hand. "When they dope me up, the Jesus gets so small, Henry. I keep expecting him to disappear altogether."

My grandfather cleared his throat.

"Then we'd have a white space right in the middle of everything. What would we do then, Henry?"

Papa gave a relieved smile, as if he'd already considered such a scenario, that Jesus might someday dwindle away to nothing, and leave the wall gaping. "Gore. How would you like that, Geraldine? We could put up a nice one of Al Gore."

The old woman's eyes cleared then, and for a moment she was the woman who had played catch with me in the yard when I was small, winding up and stinging it into the pocket of my mitt; the woman who cried, "Is that my devil-toed grandchild?" when I answered the telephone; the woman who sat at my grandfather's right hand, and demanded that the flunkies from the corporate office give the workers their fair share, or else their board of directors might as well just pull up a few lawn chairs and watch the pigeons crap on the dry-docked skeleton of their aircraft carrier until it turned completely white.

Nana squeezed Papa's hand, and at same time, met my eyes with a knowing, mirthful gaze. "Do you think this mean Al Gore died for our sins, darling?"

And that was how a photograph of Al Gore had come to take Jesus' coveted position to the left of Joseph Hillstrom, and the Son of God had been relegated to a spot above the light switch.

The next day, as I took my turn in the rifle seat and Papa stretched out on the bed, I contemplated the odd juxtaposition of the clean-cut politician in his navy blue suit, and the hatchet-faced convict in the high collar.

If you think that Al Gore would have rolled back NAFTA, turn to page 32. If you think that Joseph Hillstrom could eat Al Gore's gizzard with a smile on his face, turn to page 44.

I looked away, flipped up the edge of the orange curtain. Except for a single squirrel, painstakingly dismantling an acorn in the shade of the hedge, nothing moved. A shiny blue pickup came around the bend, and disappeared a dozen yards later around the edge of my grandparents' roof. I dropped the curtain. From the bed, Papa's breath came shallow.

"Papa," I said.

He didn't answer. He was asleep. Maybe it was better that way. There was something I wanted to ask, just say out loud, just to try on. His hands were folded in his lap.

"Doesn't it seem like—Joseph Hillstrom—with the gun, and with the bullet wound, and the mystery woman thing—doesn't it seem like—"

"—No." His voice was clear and hard; it was like a voice a behind my ear, and I jumped a little in my seat.

"No?"

"Suspicion is not proof, George. Suspicion is never proof. 'Suspicion' is how they see things the way they want to see them. It's an excuse for cracking down. Bosses use it, cops use it. Presidents use it. And it counts for nothing." His hands lay still on his belt buckle and his eyes remained closed.

Then what about Steven Sugar? What have you got him besides suspicion? I wrote on my legal pad. If my summer of correspondence had taught me anything, it was that it was easier to be a smartass when you didn't have to use your mouth.

I turned over the corner of the curtain to see an aqua-colored sports car round the corner. "You're right about the blue cars," I said, tore off the sheet, and crumpled it up in my pocket.

Late that afternoon, we switched positions, and I drowsed off on the bed. I jerked awake at the champagne pop of the rifle, and the sound of Papa cursing, "Goddammit!"

We rushed downstairs, and out to the lawn.

The squirrel lay twitching in the grass, in a pool of red paint. The paintball had hit him in the head; his neck appeared terribly twisted, corkscrewed almost. The animal's limbs fluttered and swam in the paint, as if it were trying to dig itself out of something, sand or mud, but just kept sinking.

Papa ran a hand through his hair. "I saw him out of the corner of my eye, George. It was—reflex."

The squirrel stopped moving and a little while later I dug a grave in the backyard with my grandmother's trowel. Gil crutched over with his peppermint tin. He rolled a joint, but my grandfather took a pass. "I feel like shit, Gil. A squirrel, for God's sake."

"Back in Nam, I believe this is what they called 'collateral damage.'"

"Yup," I said. I knew all about it.

"Oh, shit," said Papa. "Shit, shit, shit."

Gil fired up the spliff. In the cooling twilight, the dirty burn of the cannabis mixed with the deep green scent of the full summer trees, and produced a carnival smell, sweaty and sweet at the same time.

My grandfather tamped the turned ground with the toe of his shoe. He shook his head. He had been shaking his head almost continuously since we found the paint-spattered body.

"But it's not as though you shot the president, Henry. It is just a squirrel," said Gil.

"It's a travesty is what it is," said Papa. He went inside, and slammed the sliding door shut.

Gil raised an eyebrow at me. He leaned on his walker and extended the smoldering joint. "Toke?"

I shook my head. I was curious, and not overly self-aware, but drugs never seemed worth it. "When people in my family get high, they get arrested. Or pregnant at eighteen."

"Or they kill squirrels," said Gil, and winked at me as he helped himself to a long, hard draw on the spliff.

When I left to go home, Papa was in the bathroom, blowing his nose very hard and running the faucet.

5.

The following morning, we reconnoitered in Papa's Buick. Gil drove the Skylark in slow loops through the dozen blocks of their north Amberson neighborhood while I sat in the front and watched to make sure he didn't drowse off. Papa sat in the rear with the rifle under a blanket at his feet. My grandfather hoped that we might catch Steven Sugar unawares, and beat him at his own game.

We undertook these missions in the afternoons, when the well-kept row houses were either empty for the workday, or curtained against the heat. A few sprinklers swepts back and forth, and on the lawn of one local eccentric, a rank of glitzy whirligigs detected a faint wind, but the majority of movement was limited to the heat snakes that curled up from the macadam.

"Henry, you realize that we've transformed into disaffected young black men? Armed gang members who cruise the streets for their enemies? The parallel is unavoidable." Gil made this remark as he steered us past the whirligig house.

It had been over a week since Steven Sugar spray-painted **COMMUNIST SHITHEEL!** across Al Gore's face in hot pink, the longest interval between attacks so far. July had melted into August. As the miniature windmills stirred, they spilled colored speckles across the road.

"I'm not complaining, mind you," said Gil, "I actually kind of like being a disaffected young black man." He gave me a bloodshot sidelong wink.

Papa took a peanut from the can in his lap and popped it in his mouth. My grandfather wore the kind of sunglasses that are given out at an optometrist's office to protect a patient's dilated eyes: a pair of filmy orange squares.

Gil's eyes fluttered and his head nodded. The Skylark drifted left. I shook his shoulder, and he snapped up straight. "You know, Henry, like in the rap music. Compton and South Central. Long Beach."

"Like a drive-by," I said.

"Old school," said Gil.

"It's not the same," my grandfather said, finally unable to contain himself.

"It's not?"

"We're not out to kill the little shit. That's the difference. We're sending a message."

"The methodology's the same. It's a hit, Henry."

"No, it is not." Papa stomped his foot several times in the backseat well. "It is not."

We drove past a postage stamp of a park, a tetherball with no ball, a slide, a few benches, and trees. A tabby cat lay on its belly in the grass, waiting for a pigeon to get careless.

"Back when I was organizing," Papa began, and I had to stare down at my shoes to conceal a smile. This opening gambit was one of my mother's favorite pieces of shorthand, our family's equivalent of the "When I was a boy, I had to walk to school . . ." speech.

If I complained about the too soft spray of the showerhead in our latest apartment my mother was wont to say, *Back when I was organizing,* and sounding her best and gruffest Papa imitation, *we considered ourselves lucky indeed if, on occasion, the company goon squads deigned to release us from our cages to bathe in a rainstorm.*

The grin was still curling the corners of my mouth when I glanced up and caught sight of Papa in the rearview mirror. For an instant, a trick of refraction briefly caused the skin of his cheap sunglasses to warp translucent; and I saw that my grandfather's eyes were locked on me. I quickly cast my gaze away. We took a right onto a new street, like the other streets, houses and grass and pavement.

He continued: "We never lost a fight. Because we knew it was a fight. When some scab crossed the line, he was kicking another guy's kid right in the face, tearing the clothes right off another man's wife, burning down his house. That's a goddamn fight." He stomped his foot again, and this time his optometrist's sunglasses slid off his nose and down into the well.

For a few seconds he scrabbled around for them. Then there was a crinkle of plastic and a grunt of triumph. Papa sat up, and I looked in the rearview mirror to see that the sunglasses had been restored, but the thin orange lenses were dented now, as if someone had clocked him. He sat breathing hard for several seconds.

When my grandfather spoke again, he sounded oddly sedated. "I'll give you an example," he said, and then he told us about Tom Hellweg.

My grandfather, Henry McGlaughlin, grew up with Tom Hellweg in Bangor, a city in the northern part of the state. They had lived on the same street, and once broke their legs together. This was in a sledding accident on Drummond Street Hill when they were both thirteen, only a couple of years younger than I was now. The steepest road in town, Drummond scaled all the way up from the bank of the Penobscot River to the residential hills where the long-departed lumber barons of the nineteenth century built their mansions with fortunes made on the backs of unorganized sawyers and lumberjacks.

It was in one of these Victorians—which like many of the great manors of the previous century had by that time been carved into a baroque and unheatable boardinghouse—that a half century after the last log spun down the Penobscot, the two boys came to know each other.

They made an obvious pair, Tom and Henry, if for no other reason than because of their fathers, or rather, their lack of fathers. Tom lost his in the mud of Amiens, and knew nothing of the man but the single gaiter that had been shipped home and sat in the place of honor on the mantelpiece, right beneath the crucifix. Henry's father wasn't dead, but Old Renny McGlaughlin had been in a threshing accident, and spent his days on a stool in the Whig & Courier, silently sipping black beer, with his stump propped on the neighboring stool so folks knew to stay away.

Tom and Henry walked to school together; they played ball together and fished together and made lists of the things they would buy with the money they made robbing banks together; they used a pulley system to send notes back and forth between Tom's second-floor window and Henry's first-floor window; and after they filled the gaiter on the mantelpiece with daffodils and cattails, when Mrs. Hellweg came home, the two boys were marched out into the yard together, and ordered to break off each other's switches.

In other words, they were the kind of boys—the kind of friends—who looked out at the great, ice-sheathed roller coaster of Drummond Street Hill one Sunday morning in February, and both saw that it wasn't road at all, but an enormous, shiny black tongue, *na-na-nah-nah-ing* at them, like a bully.

They lugged their two-man toboggan out into the freezing rain and along the sidewalk until they came to the crest of the hill. A half inch of black ice coated the road, and the cutbacks and swoops glittered all the way down to Valley Avenue.

For a minute, they sat in the chute, their hands on the cold ground beside the runners, taking in the massive drop. It was a mile to the bottom, maybe two miles, maybe ten. At the foot of the hill, a hundred yards beyond the road's end, the Penobscot River poured between the snowy banks, streaming dark and bobbing with slabs of ice.

"You know, this is how my dad really lost his leg," said Henry, and slapped the blade of one of the toboggan's runners.

Tom turned to look at him.

"Cut him clean off at the knee."

Tom bit his lip. He scratched his forehead.

Henry cackled.

"You bastard," said Tom, and kicked off.

Henry clutched Tom around the waist, expecting the rush of speed that carried them the first few yards, but not the takeoff that ripped the toboggan clean from its rails. His mouth opened in a scream and he was thrown forward. His teeth sank into the back of Tom's head. The dark green on the pine trees streaked across the slate gray of the sky and he tasted his friend's hair and his sweat and his blood. Wind shot through his clothes; his jacket ballooned with air; he flew.

At the bottom, in a snowbank more than a hundred feet beyond the crossing of Drummond and Valley, they came to rest in a pile of tinder. Tom's right leg had twisted with Henry's left; blood speckled the snow; the icy drizzle fell on their bare heads, their caps torn away or maybe disintegrated.

"We were a mile from home, and it was below zero, and we both had the same fracture, a clean break at the shin, and did it hurt? It goddamn hurt." Addressing me in the rearview mirror, Papa opened his mouth and pointed at a discolored incisor. "And this, too. I lost the tooth, and he had it sticking in the back of his head. You think that hurt a little?"

And the first thing Tom said was, "Do you think we can put the toboggan back together again? It won't be this good for long."

To which Henry said, "I don't think we can put it back together again, but I bet we can borrow one."

And the two boys leaned against each other, sharing legs, Henry's right and Tom's left, taking turns, one foot after another to get home.

"That's how far and deep I went back with that son-of-a-bitch Tom Hellweg."

So far and deep that, twenty years after Tom Hellweg's family moved to New Hampshire and the last time Henry saw him, when the former appeared on the latter's doorstep one morning and asked for a job, Henry never even paused. "For Christ's sake, Tom, put your hat back on. We're going to be late for work."

A full-time position in the painting shop was assigned to Tom Hellweg before the day was out, and by the time the quitting bell rang, a group of men on their days off had already moved his wife and three children into an apartment house.

The matter of his friend's felony record—eight months upstate for running a bait-and-switch telephone scam hustling Quebecois migrants into wiring emergency money to their gravely sick *mères* back home in the province—a felony being a strict prohibitive in the strongest union in Maine, was no prohibitive at all to Henry McGlaughlin. Henry believed in second chances, and Tom Hellweg was a man who had once propped him up, and borne his weight as if it were his own.

That the Tom he knew had matured into a gaunt, raccoon-eyed malingerer capable of bilking people so poor they made their shoes out of potatoes was something Henry refused to consider. Neither did he permit himself to disapprove of his old friend for, besides being the slowest worker in his shop, ritualistically painting the word **CUNT** into every plate and board that came before his brush, and then filling in from there. The only thing that mattered was that the work got done, and after all, someone had to be the slowest. Henry also chose to overlook Tom's drinking, and his habit of sitting apart from other men at lunchtime; and although it was a struggle, he even kept it to himself when someone told him that the Hellweg children collected handfuls of cigarette butts out of street gutters and brought them home for their father. Some men drank; some men liked to eat alone; and some men had their own ideas about raising their children.

And Tom was his friend, goddamn it. That was something you never forgot. That was the essence of decency.

"That was what the union was about," said Papa.

Gil cleared his throat.

My grandfather cut him off before he could start. "Not a word, you. Just keep driving."

A few months passed, however, and a situation arose regarding his old friend that Henry could not ignore. Henry received a report that Tom, on two occasions, both well after midnight, had blithely asked other workers to give him a lift from a local bar to the pipefitting shop on the Ironworks campus, because he wanted to see "how they had things set up." Tom said he was thinking of putting together a workshop himself, at home, you see, and he just wondered how they had things arranged.

These reports matched up with another set of reports, from the morning foreman of the pipefitting shop, who found tools scattered around along with signs that someone had been welding after hours.

"What's that sound like to you, Gerry?" Henry asked his wife. He didn't look up from the table.

"Cross-training," said Geraldine McGlaughlin, and went to retrieve the bottle from the cabinet. She poured two straight.

This came at a time when Local 219, like every other union in the country, found itself in a battle to find some kind of higher ground in the wake of the Taft-Hartley debacle. After fifty years of struggle and progress, the Taft-Hartley Act had served notice to the entire movement that the cripple was buried in Hyde Park and the men who inherited the family monopolies were back in charge—and they had the veto-proof Congress to prove it. In the name of free trade, Taft-Hartley's deregulations had kicked the Communists out of the movement, limited the unions' power to strike, and above all else, pinched off the increasing influence of organized labor over middle management positions.

It was one thing for the commoners to organize, Taft-Hartley seemed to say, but it was quite another for such things to get out into the greater community, where men wore ties and worked at desks. That wouldn't do at all.

And it was this last point that should have resulted in Local 219's complete unawareness of the midnight shop work, because this group of low-level white-collar workers most certainly included all of the foremen of the Amberson Ironworks, the on-site representatives who filed the reports to New York. Except—

—Except that upon the passage of Taft-Hartley, Henry McGlaughlin had, much more quickly than most, gauged the new lay of the land, and taken preemptive action. That is to say, in the best interest of his constituents, Henry immediately began giving a select group of Ironworks' foremen a monthly token of Local 219's appreciation—a very modest bribe. Along with this cash subsidy, in 1952, it may still have meant something to these managers that Henry was a fellow like them, who lived in a house like theirs, and not in some apartment in New York City with twelve-foot windows overlooking Central Park, and a bathroom with one of those gold-plated sinks to wash your ass.

Or, as Gerry put it when she visited the wives of these managers every third Monday afternoon to present the crisp ten-dollar bill that promised their husband's loyalty, "You know we're all in the same boat, honey."

Nonetheless, as Local 219 flouted the direction of the Taft-Hartley wind, and demanded new safety regulations and full benefits for a dozen part-time hires, Henry McGlaughlin had lately been much concerned; the *Lewiston Sun-Times* reported that several unidentified sources promised that a lockout was inevitable.

"We [company officials] don't like it [Local 219]," says one anonymous source. "Those people [the workers] have been given an inflated sense of self-importance. It's bad for them [the workers], and it's bad for business. We're not running a socialist enterprise here. We plan to re-establish the chain of command. We need workers who want to work, do their jobs. What we don't need are whiners, reds, and other undesirables that the unions typically carry along and suckle."

All of which leant Tom Hellweg's unauthorized after-hour's visits to the pipefitting shop a particularly suspicious appearance. It was a well-known scheme among downsizing companies to cross-train workers, to teach them how to do more than one skilled task, so that in the case of a sudden layoff production would not be affected. The problem, of course, was that while production would not be affected, the men who lost their jobs and the families of those men would most certainly be affected.

After a second glass with his wife, this one with a bit of ice, Henry McGlaughlin went off to find his old friend, Tom Hellweg. He went off to ask Tom—formerly the boy with whom he tamed the black roller coaster of Drummond Street Hill, the boy who bore Henry's weight as if it were his own—just what was going on.

Or, as Henry McGlaughlin put it then, "What the fuck are you up to here, Tommy?"

Tom stood at his station in the painting shop. He stared at Henry from beneath drooping eyelids, a crocodile stare, the one that says that the crocodile would eat you, if only the meal weren't so paltry as to make the effort redundant. Tom spat a tiny cigarette butt out onto the floor, probably one that his children had picked from a gutter so that he could get another three drags out of it.

"Well, speak up, Tommy," Henry said. "I'm asking you a question."

Tom turned back to the section of metal plating that he was spraying with red industrial paint, and carefully spelled the word "**HENRY**." Over the top of this word, he then wrote the word "**CUNT**."

"No," said Tom. "I'm asking you a question, Mr. McGlaughlin: just what the fuck do you think you are doing?"

Then his old friend plucked another grimy butt from his pocket. Tom lit it, turned his back on his union representative, and returned to work.

*   *   *

From that point, the plot unraveled with the craven simplicity that was considered standard business practice among the upstanding board members in New York and D.C., whose knowledge of the Amberson Ironworks extended only as far as the third column of numbers on a monthly profit sheet.

A cursory investigation revealed that a stranger, a gentleman from Boston who carried his cigarettes in an ivory case, had in recent weeks spread around a great many free drinks in the local pubs. Among the stranger's drinking partners had been several members of Local 219—including Tom Hellweg.

Acting on this tip, Gerry called the Portland hotel where the stranger with the ivory cigarette case was said to be staying. She spoke in a deep baritone, and started to badger the desk clerk before he could even say hello: "This is Mr. Fink, Chief Officer of the East Coast Branch of the Pinkerton Detective Agency, and I need to speak to my man immediately. I don't know what name he's using, you can never be too careful when you're dealing with the sort of riffraff we deal with in this business, but he's been charging the room to a company account, and I really must speak to him right away."

The jolted desk clerk quickly rifled through his ledger. "Do you mean Edgar Hallsworthy in room sixteen? Oh, but wait a minute: he's charging his room to an account belonging to St. Cloud Detective Agency—"

"—That's right," Mr. Fink cut him off. "That's exactly right. He's from the St. Cloud arm of our operation. Now put me straight through to Hallsworthy."

A moment later, the clerk connected him to room sixteen, and a man with a Brahmin accent answered. Gerry asked if he had sent down four shirts to the laundry. The cheerful Brahmin-voiced man said, "Wrong room, sweets. I don't go around trusting my linen to just any old chink, you know." She apologized, and rung off.

"So?" asked Henry.

Gerry shook her head and went to refill the glasses, but the bottle was empty.

Henry put his foremen on alert, and by the end of the week

peered after us, and although the distance hooded his eyes, I could feel them boring into me. Steven Sugar seemed larger than I remembered him from the previous school year, lengthened somehow, drawn upward like the flag.

Perched on the back of his partner's shoulders, Tolson made a rifle from his naked arms and sighted us.

We swung into the bend and they were gone. They knew. They knew my grandfather. They knew us. Knew me. The realization was like a baby's hand, suddenly squeezing my stomach with tiny fingers.

The Skylark dipped over the hill and the mall disappeared.

"I don't want to shoot anybody today, George," said Gil, under his breath. "This stuff is crazy. Your grandfather's not thinking clearly. He thinks people are out to get him. He needs to relax. Forget about the Sunday *New York Times* and forget about Al Gore. None of it's worth it. Like the old Jew said, 'We're all just pawns in their game.'"

He pulled the car into the driveway. Papa mumbled in his sleep. I got out and fetched Gil's walker from the trunk, then held his bony elbow as he doddered to his feet.

"All this stress over politics? Over a politician? Over Al Gore? Does that make sense to you, George?"

In the high noon light his bald head and his round, smooth face appeared as if they were carved from wax.

I shrugged.

Gil settled into his walker with a grunt of satisfaction. "Of course it doesn't. For heaven's sake—and I'd appreciate it if we kept this between us—but a man of your grandfather's beliefs should be saying good riddance to Gore. Four years of Bush and maybe people will have suffered enough to elect a man of real principle. Someone with a few more inches in the crotch department if you get my drift."

He saw me scratch my head. Gil said, "Now, now. I didn't say the N word, George, don't worry. I didn't say Nader."

"You just did," I pointed out.

Gil put a finger to his nostril and winked.

When I started to see him to the sidewalk, he waved me off. "Go on and help your grandfather, George. I'll be fine. I just want to go home and smoke a joint and take a nap. And maybe if I'm feeling ambitious, I'll try to screw my wife, but that's it."

He scraped forward a couple of feet and stopped. His back was to me. "See anybody?" he asked.

I spun around, expecting to see Sugar right behind me, Tolson on his shoulders, scowling like a gargoyle. The street was empty of traffic and the driveway of the house across the street unoccupied. The day was hot and still, broken only by the distant wails from the public pool. Inside the Buick, Papa snorted in his sleep.

I exhaled. "No."

"Good." Gil started to fumble with something I couldn't see.

"Gil? Are you okay?"

He answered with a deep, hitching sigh. There was a trickle as he began to urinate onto the driveway. A yellow rivulet made its way along a crack in the pavement.

I stood, slightly unnerved, not sure where to put my eyes. Any car that came along . . .

Gil seemed to read my thoughts. "At my age, George, when you get the feeling, you can't mess around. You have to whip it out."

"Yeah," I said, and reminded myself that he was dying. When you were dying, you could do anything you wanted, I guessed.

In the car, Papa slept on. I opened the door to wake him. He sat with his head back, mouth wide open, so that his breath came in a wet rasp. His left hand trembled in his lap while his right rested peacefully on the butt of the IL-47. Maybe he was dreaming sweetly of my grandmother; maybe he was dreaming of Steven Sugar, of the surprise that would be on the kid's face when a paintball stung the back of his naked ear, the red paint stippling his hair like real blood; or maybe Papa was just dreaming of old friends.

I thought of how Gil saw the world, rotten straight through, and until people were ready to start over again, a joint and a nap were about the best you could get. My grandfather, on the other hand, saw life as a war, and if you didn't martial your forces, if you didn't shoot first, they might start just by taking the Travel section of your Sunday *New York Times*, or spray-painting your property, or making you wear a yellow star, but in the end, they would take everything, then hand you a shovel.

It seemed to me that the old men were both correct in their own way, that their points of view were parallel islands of inviolable truth. My feet, spread very wide, were planted on each. I knew that no resistance could achieve what I wanted; but I also knew that except for resistance, I had nothing at all.

I put a hand on my grandfather's shoulder and shook him until he opened his eyes.

Afterward, I killed an hour or so at the library crinkling through a summer of Sundays. I perused the Travel sections and the Style sections of the Sunday *New York Times*. I wanted to understand why Steven Sugar had needed to take them. Sunlight fell through the bank of leaded windows by the reading table, warming my left ear and gilding the colored front pages.

Here were far lands and beautiful sights; here were the new ways people were living and here were the announcements of marriage. I followed the lines with my finger and studied the photographs of vistas and smiling faces, but the sunlight distracted me. Outside, seated on a bench, a girl with red hair and a blue peasant blouse was alternately reading a paperback and using her fingertip to apply layer upon layer of lip gloss. One of her bra straps hung loose around her white shoulder. I could make out the shine of dampness at her throat.

My attention wandered between the newspaper and the girl, scanning the columns and tracking her finger as it lapped around and around her mouth. Later, I would find myself able to remember only two articles, both—unsurprisingly—with a sexual content: the first, a travel piece about Rhodes, and the second, a report on the culture of elderly swingers.

The travel article was by a professor who had visited the island of Rhodes after each of his four divorces. The professor wrote that he felt an interminable sadness in the city, in the great abandoned keeps and twisty avenues of the Old Town. The Crusaders had built this place and been vanquished without a fight. So, in his sadness, he took comfort in the failures of other committed men. The professor liked to imagine that the last Knights of St. John had somehow been transformed into the swarms of stray cats who haunted the cornices, licked ice cream off the cobblestones, and baked themselves on the rock walls above the beach, in view of the nude sunbathers. If the Army of God could resign itself to such simple gratifications, the professor wrote, he believed he could love again.

In the Style section I was enthralled—and not a little mortified—by a report on the challenges, and the dangers, faced by aging swingers. Viagra didn't work for everyone, and for some it worked too well: men threw out their backs; one woman, her skull cracked against a headboard, suffered a concussion and a lingering case of vertigo. "I'm not sure if I'm sexually aroused or just obstinate," a retired stockbroker was quoted saying at one senior orgy. He was described as being seated on a piano bench, wearing only black socks and garters. "No matter what, though," said the man. "It's nice to be among your peers. No one here is going to be doing it standing up, that's for sure."

But I found myself drowsing between paragraphs, and stole glances at the red-haired girl on the grass, both of us distracted by her mouth. I rested my head down on the union of a theater director and a bank vice-president, and traced a lazy fingertip along the cool ridge of a leaded window.

The clap of the hand against glass snapped me straight. The legs of my chair scraped back with a shriek of protest. Steven Sugar, cheeks flushed and eyes wide, stood on the other side of the window. Pressed flush against the glass, his meaty hand was inches from my face.

He leaned forward until his nose touched the glass. I could see the scraggly black hairs poking from his chin and the tornados of freckles under his eyes.

"Can you hear me?" he asked, his voice deadened but clear.

Yes, I mouthed.

"Speak up," said Sugar.

"Yes," I said.

"I've seen you driving around with the geezers. Old Man McGlaughlin, he's your grandfather, ain't he?"

"Uh-huh," I said.

"Tell him I didn't take his newspapers."

"Okay," I said.

Steven Sugar flared his nostrils, nodded to himself. He took a step back, still glaring at me.

Then, suddenly, he jumped forward, smearing his face up against the glass and knocking off his square-billed camouflage hat. "Tell your grandfather I will burn down his motherfucking house if he doesn't leave me alone."

Tolson, the lieutenant, appeared over Sugar's shoulder. He sneered and rapped a knuckle on the window. "Maybe we'll burn down your house, bitch."

"I will make him my own private Vietnam," said Steven Sugar. "You got that, kid? I will make you all my very own private fucking Vietnam."

I said I had it.

"Hey, bitch. Bitch, you've got black all over you," said Tolson and patted his cheek.

They turned and walked to where their bikes leaned against a tree. Sugar spun around, shot a thick finger at me, and then climbed on his bike. They rode across the park to the street and disappeared into traffic.

In the bathroom I splashed water on my face, and scrubbed the newspaper ink off my cheek.

I paused on the front steps of the library, blinking at the high, late-afternoon sun. My skin prickled at the sudden change in heat and humidity from the cool, dry confines of the library. I still wasn't quite awake. The encounter with Steven Sugar and his lieutenant had a fuzzy, dreamlike quality in my mind, although I knew it had been real.

I put a hand over my eyes and scanned the park to see if they were waiting for me. I remembered asking Papa what I was, and how he had said I was his "henchman." In Mafia movies, when there was a gangland war, the dons often sent each other's dead henchman back and forth like letters. I imagined Tolson sitting on Sugar's shoulders and running my corpse up the flagpole in front of the sporting goods store.

The park was empty, though; even the red-haired girl with the lips was gone.

"Hey, you! Hey, sexy!"

The voice came from behind me and I took an involuntary step forward, the sole of my sneaker slipping on the slick marble. I teetered for a moment, about to fall face first. She grabbed my shoulder and I threw out my hand. I caught hold of something small and spongy and cloth covered, and steadied myself.

The red-haired girl cleared her throat, laughed.

I removed my hand from where it clutched her breast. Heat spilled across my face.

"You surprised me," I said. "I reached out."

"Yes, you did," she said.

For something to say, I blinked several times at the space over her right shoulder.

"I'm Myrna Carp," said the red-haired girl and stuck her hand out. "And you must be George." She was eighteen or nineteen, I figured.

We shook. She had damp little hands.

"George," she said again, and shook her head and giggled. I halfway expected her to whip out a stick, throw it, and tell me to fetch. I probably would have.

Myrna had a crooked way of smiling, like she was one up on you before you even talked. Of course, Myrna Carp was one up on me; she already knew my name.

"How—?"

"—I worked for Planned Parenthood second semester. I was your mother's intern. Emma's got a photo of you right on her desk, you know? Of you in your Little League uniform? Number twenty-five? Tri-City Auto Parts? Very sharp, my friend."

"Hey, you know, that photo's a couple of years old," I said.

Myrna leaned back slightly and gave me a look of open appraisal. Then she smiled at me with her funny jagged smile, as if she had determined that I was a charming, but very fake diamond.

"I can see that. You're much taller in real life. And you didn't have sideburns then, right?"

To the best of my knowledge, this was the first time someone had deemed to call the wispy curls at my temples sideburns.

"Anyway, I just recognized you, and, man, George, did you know that your mom is fucking awesome?"

"Yeah," I said, swallowing down the lump in my throat. "Sure."

"Your mom wrote me the most kick-ass recommendation, which is probably the only reason I got into Vassar. She also talked my frigging mother into letting me get on the pill, which is probably the only reason I didn't have to kill anybody senior year of high school.

"Your mom is my dogg." Myrna Carp laughed and ran a hand back through her red hair. "My dogg. Jesus, listen to me, huh?"

Something in my face made her rewind. "Well, I'm sure it's a little different for you. Being as she's your mom and all." There was an expectant pause. The library doors hissed open as a man bustled out with an armload of books, and a gust of air-conditioning washed over me.

"Did I just tell you that your mother helped me get on the pill?" I nodded.

She put a hand over her face and peeked at me between her fingers. "I've embarrassed you, haven't I?"

"No, no," I said. "No, really."

Myrna cocked her head and squinted at me.

"Really," I said again, a little desperately.

Her gaze relaxed, but still held me, green eyes fading to amber as she leaned forward into the bright patch of sun that lay between us. She reached out and grabbed my shoulders. Then, slowly, she drew me into her chest and embraced me. A moment passed. I hugged back. Myrna sighed. "People should say hello like this," she said, and kissed my forehead.

Myrna broke away, spun and took the stairs in two big steps, and skipped away. "Nice to meet you, George! You're even cuter than in your pictures," she called over her shoulder. "And tell your mother I love her!"

*   *   *

So I'm polydactyl; I have six toes on my right foot. Only about one or two in every thousand people have a condition like mine. It's a genetic tendency, something I have from my father's side of the family. As a toe, it's not much more than a pink nub at the far edge of my foot. My extra toe looks like something that just kind of crawled on, and stuck; the nail is nothing but a dab of gloss. My grandmother used to tease me about it. Nana called it my "devilish toe." Papa liked to say it made me a freak. "It proves you're one of us," he said.

I once asked my mother if I could have it removed. When I put this question forth, I was sitting on the cracked linoleum of the kitchen floor in our apartment in Farmington, clutching a piece of coarse sandpaper.

My mother raised an interrogatory eyebrow.

"I thought I might be able to sand it off," I said. At the time I was only a kid, ten years old.

Of course, Emma said.

Two scrapes, however, had reduced me to tears. The devilish toe was tiny, but it was really attached, no doubt about that.

She sat down across from me Indian style, and put her hands on my knees. Then, she asked me why, and I told her the obvious thing, because of my father. "I don't want any part of him."

The last few days had been hard. Somehow or other, my father had obtained our phone number. "Who is this?" he had asked when I answered the first time. "Is that you, George? Is that you? It's your dad, it's your old man." A moment passed. The only sound I could manage to produce was a humming noise. My father started to laugh, and then he broke into wrenching sobs. "Say something, George. Can't you fucking say something to your old man? Or are you too fucking good?"

Since then, we had just been letting the telephone ring. Sometimes it rang for twenty minutes. The jingles hit me like screaming voices. I had wet myself having a nightmare about a man with a glistening black telephone for a head. The man with the telephone head had scrabbled up the stone blocks of a well, like some awful spider, and I couldn't seem to back away.

"I hate it," I said and slapped my foot, slapped the sad lump of my extra toe that was already raw and sore.

Emma nodded. Her face wore the peaceful expression of a cemetery angel—mournful, but carved with the assurance that no further harm can come.

Suppose, she said, that a birth defect is like a work-related injury.

"Like when Papa's dad lost his leg in the thresher?"

My mother rolled her eyes at me. Yes, she said, but without the blood and guts, my beautiful little psychopath.

Now, she went on, you got an extra toe on the job. So you turned to your Workers Comp, because you were organized and had benefits and so forth.

"Naturally," I said. By age ten I was well versed in such necessities.

But your injury is different, George, because you didn't lose anything. She stressed this point, staring hard. You gained something. You have something more. You're not handicapped at all.

"Well then, how am I getting Comp?" I asked.

My mother took a deep breath. There's a special clause in the life contract for workers who are born with extra toes, she said. Comp applies to them even though the extra toe isn't detrimental.

"That sounds like featherbedding," I said. "My union is going to be under investigation if it isn't careful."

She looked at me.

"Okay," I said. "But it's just a toe. A toe can't do shit."

It's a gift, Emma said, it's a gift. And Workers Comp insured you while you learned to utilize that gift, and afterward the union found you another job. Some task your special gift is uniquely suited for.

And watch your language, she added.

I touched my toe. It was barely anything; it was half of a chunky french fry; it could not possibly have a function.

"What task?"

She shrugged. We're still in the rehabilitation stage, she said. I'm your Workers Comp, by the way, Emma added. Roughly speaking, that's what mothers provide for kids. They rehabilitate them for life.

I studied my toe. It was nothing.

You'll see, she said. It'll come in handy.

Then my mother said, I love you. Then she said, And he loves you. He does love you.

The phone started to ring, and we sat on the floor of the kitchen for a while longer without saying anything.

At the time of my conception in the spring of 1985, Ty Claiborne held a good union job, as a movie theater projectionist at the Amberson Pavilion Two. This was how Emma McGlaughlin, the daughter of the local union heads, Henry and Geraldine McGlaughlin, happened to meet him. It was her first summer job, and Ty Claiborne—tall and broad and possessed of the crinkled, soulful gaze of a much older man—was her first real crush. He carried his pack of Lucky Strikes rolled up in the sleeve of his black T-shirt and wore huge sunglasses, like a state trooper. I wish he'd pull me over, Emma told her friends.

If, however, a week into the summer, the Northeastern Projectionists Union had not gone on strike, maybe things would never have gone beyond a crush stage—but the theater chain told the union to take it or leave it, and the projectionists walked in June. So it was in the spirit of unity that Emma promptly quit her summer job, and whipped up a big batch of pot brownies to lift the spirits of her fellow workers.

Ten years older, Ty drove a car that was almost new, rented his own apartment, had painstakingly collected every album Bob Dylan had ever recorded—*on vinyl*. Ty Claiborne could also put away a whole mess of pot brownies. In her teenage bedroom, Emma's poster of River Phoenix rubbed shoulders with a magazine clipping of Woody Guthrie posing with his "This Machine Kills Fascists" guitar; she never had a chance. Ty seemed like the perfect combination of both, a dreamboat and a union man.

What Ty Claiborne did not seem like was a man with a drinking problem. Nor did he seem like a man with a cocaine addiction, or a man who would very soon be forced to sell his complete collection of Dylan records to support that addiction. He did not seem like a man on the verge of his third strike with the Northeastern Projectionists Union, or a man three months in arrears on his rent, or a man who would lift cash from his seventeen-year-old girlfriend's Minnie Mouse leatherette purse. Perhaps above all other things, Ty Claiborne did not seem like the sort of man who would use a condom that he found in the sleeve of a thrift store copy of *Another Side of Bob Dylan* (a condom with an expiration date clearly printed on the back, 3/1/66), and who would still use said condom after carrying it around in his tool pouch for weeks, along with the ring of screwdrivers and pins that he used for projector maintenance. He was, however, all of these things—and so, of course, it was lucky for me that my mother didn't know.

But in the fifteen years since, we had both learned plenty about my father. For instance, there were lessons about bankruptcy, about creditors, about rehab, and about the cost of collect calls between the hours of three and five A.M. Once, in the parking lot outside our apartment in Blue Hill, we learned that laid-back Paul Bagley— hippie potter, borderline narcoleptic, and Green Party stalwart, Paul Bagley—was capable of disarming a strung-out junkie ex-husband wielding a Swiss Army knife, and then of beating the wretch unconscious with a snow shovel. We learned about restraining orders.

Meanwhile, my father discovered that he could maintain his fix by stealing cars, but one night in Lewiston he learned that it was a bad idea to pass out while idling in a stolen BMW in the drive-through line at Arby's. After that my mother and I learned that when someone sent you a letter from a maximum security prison, the envelope was sliced open by an administration official and perused for obscenity, threats, incrimination, or anything else that might be interesting, before it was taped shut and sent along for delivery.

And somewhere along the line, I became self-educated in the indispensable mechanism of pure wishfulness, and I began to fantasize of a Real Father, a superhero, unavoidably delayed by matters related to the security of the universe. This was the kind of father I needed, because only the planets and the stars were important enough to forgive for putting us through all this.

*   *   *

Now, as I rode home with Myrna Carp's college girl lips still printed on my forehead, the old despair tickled at the back of my neck. It had never really left, I knew. That feeling was as much a part of me as my extra toe; it was attached.

I told myself that college was full of beautiful girls, beautiful girls who had not shared their reproductive concerns with my mother. At a place like Vassar College—wherever that was, and whatever it was—I bet they practically fell down out of the sky, like rain. I bet at Vassar College you needed to wear an army helmet to deflect all the gorgeous, precipitating girls, and the birth control pills pinging down like hail. I told myself that she had liked me.

Unconvinced, I pedaled down Route 12 with a hard-on and a feeling of general gloom. I imagined Myrna Carp falling nude through the sky, and landing, with a squeal of joy and a pillowy bounce of her breasts, onto the broad shoulders of Steven Sugar. "Let's raise the flag, babe," said Steven. "Oh, let's!" cried Myrna.

Then, at dinner, I almost choked on a lump of mashed potato. I started coughing and needed to drink half a glass of water to get it all down.

"You okay?" Dr. Vic asked.

"Did you ever sell a Bob Dylan record?" I hacked a fragment of potato into my napkin.

Dr. Vic scratched his head. "Pardon?"

My mother lowered her forehead to the table and sighed.

I repeated the question.

Dr. Vic said he was sure he hadn't. "I don't know as if I was ever hip enough for Bob Dylan, you know?"

"Yes," I said, relieved. "We can see that."

7.

Dr. Vic cleared his place at the table and announced he was going down to the dock. He didn't ask my mother if she wanted to come.

Shutting the sliding glass door with painstaking care, Dr. Vic slouched outside, his footfalls creaking heavily on the planks.

She remained in her seat, doodling on her legal pad. She drew a cartoon of Bob Dylan, with the incredible sixties Afro, the opaque sunglasses, the jagged nose and the dubious eyebrows, and slid it over to me.

I gave her a thumbs-up. Then I penciled a light saber into Dylan's hand. I gave him a speech bubble: *LUKE, I AM YOUR FATHER.*

Her sudden, tinkling laugh stung my eyes. *Do you want to assist me in a secret mission?*

Yes, I wrote back.

Meet me in the car. She stood up, patted my shoulder, and left to gather her things. I wiped my eyes.

Before we left, my mother loaded the trunk, and when she climbed in, I saw that she had changed into a navy tracksuit. She handed me my black windbreaker, and I put it on. This seemed promising.

We pulled onto Route 12 and passed through the quiet of Amberson at nine o'clock on a Tuesday night.

In the old brick-faced downtown—where the buildings stood together in a stately arrangement that always reminded me of the well-worn but carefully polished and soberly colored Oxford shoes that lined the bottom of Papa's wardrobe—there were signs of the recent economic downturn. The shoe store had a HUGE SALE, the art supply store had an EVERYTHING MUST GO SALE, and according to a Jimi Hendrix poster taped in the window, the head shop was SORRY: CLOSED FOREVER HONKIES! (The statement bloomed from the corner of Jimi's mouth in a psychedelic word bubble.) At the Amberson Pavilion Two, a film called *Rat Race*, about people willing to undergo any humiliation in order to win a fortune (performed by actors who were apparently willing to take any part), played on both screens. The pawnshop seemed to be doing okay.

It occurred to me that for days, my life had been narrowed to a window not much larger than the circle at the end of the IL-47's scope. Papa should get out more, I thought to myself, before everything in town goes out of business.

Some skaters were pushing themselves around the modest town square. They wore long, jingling wallet chains, and low-hanging carpenters jeans, and wove their boards in drunken circles around the WWI monument of a huddled squad of battle-weary doughboys. Parked at the curb a couple of cops sat in their cruiser and kept watch, probably listening to the Red Sox as they finished up a disaster against New York, or just started on one with Oakland.

My eyes naturally drifted upward, to a second-floor office in the squat, ten-story building that overlooked the square.

It was from this office that Dale Crispin, my mother's last ex-boyfriend, wrote, edited, and published the local weekly, the *Amberson Common*. When they were dating, I spent a number of happy hours playing cribbage in that office, and listening in wonder and admiration at the musical vulgarity of Dale's speech.

"The shoe, my young friend," I remembered him saying to me as he counted a clutch double-run to pull himself within range of the finish line, "is now on the other dick."

But in the next hand, when he mud-holed, and I won with a flush double-run, Dale threw up his hands and pronounced, "Great Scott! The shoe returneth dickward! Of all the piss-ass luck!"

Dale swept up the cards and started to shuffle. He sprayed them back and forth between his hands and directed a keen look from under the bill of his tattered Red Sox cap. Along with his twenty-year-old cap, Dale's salt-and-pepper beard seemed to exist in a permanent state of two-days' growth, which endowed him with something of the ultra-cool, imperturbable bearing of a war correspondent. Of all Emma's boyfriends, Dale had been my favorite.

"Now. Two questions haunt me, my friend:

"First, can this streak of piss-ass luck be broken with just the simple intervention of a juju priest, or am I going to need a living sacrifice? Second, do you believe that your mother would ever consent to marry someone so far below her son's station, cribbage-wise?"

This second question hung in the air.

I felt heat rise up my neck. "What—?" I asked, and the word lay on my tongue like a mouthful of spoiled food.

"I'm just throwing things out here," said Dale.

I shrugged, flicked the head of the Ross Perot bobblehead on Dale's desk. Ross nodded like an idiot. Say something, I yelled inside myself, still not sure what precisely was going on.

"What's—a juju priest?" I asked.

"Nice dodge, kiddo." Dale produced a wry grin and stuck his hat on my head. "Deal the cards, O Purveyor of Stinging Yellow Destiny."

My mother wrote something, and then passed me her legal pad and a pen flashlight.

We were waiting parked behind a Dumpster at the rear of the parking lot adjacent to the Planned Parenthood office. She had shut off the lights and the engine. From our vantage point, we could watch the area directly in front of the clinic through a vertical gap between the Dumpster and the corner of the building. So far there was nothing to see. A pair of arc lights illuminated the entrance to the lot, highlighting the chiggers that circled over the dry grass of the diamond-shaped traffic island.

I took the legal pad and the flashlight to read: *I'm going to need you to do some driving.*

I nodded at her—affirmative. Over the years, we had lived in six different apartments, a duplex, a triplex, and for a few weeks one summer in Rockland, a fourteen-foot boat where I slept in the cabin and my mother slept in an inflatable tent on deck. From the time I was tall enough to reach the pedals I was trained to sit in the double-parked car while she unloaded boxes, and to move it if another vehicle needed to pull away from the curb.

This is about the GFAs, isn't it? This was the time of night that they made their strikes. *What are we going to do?*

My mother grinned like a pirate. *You'll like it.*

I tried to return a grin of my own. I rolled down the window, caught a pungent whiff of Dumpster, and rolled it back up.

The parking lot was windless. The cloud of chiggers stretched and undulated above the grass of the traffic island. I could feel the itch of them along my spine.

My mother scratched a new message on the pad.

What are you thinking about?

This required a more complex answer than I supposed my mother might have expected—or maybe not. I was thinking about how nice it was for the two of us to be alone, doing something together that Dr. Vic didn't know about; and I was thinking of how lame and childish it was to feel that way, like a kid feels about his mother, not like a young man who would be old enough to apply for his driver's license in five months.

I was also thinking about Dale, missing him, missing the times we played cribbage in his office. This, too, was deeply, inarguably lame. After all, it wasn't like he had been a superhero or something. Dale Crispin ran a two-bit newspaper that was so cheap you wouldn't dare to wrap fish in it. Still, I felt a little sick to remember how he asked me that question and how for some reason I couldn't find an answer.

I looked at her; she looked back.

Sometimes it stunned me, stunned me like being shaken awake, to realize her youth. The face I saw now was not very different from the face that my father saw roughly sixteen years ago, maybe even as they sat in a dark car like this one. The possibility didn't strike me as incestuous. Rather, it seemed almost holy, like a magic snapshot, like some moment out of time.

What are you thinking about?

To her question, I responded with one of my own: *Why didn't you marry Dale?*

Headlights swung across the windshield, and I glanced up to see the familiar, rusted blue minivan turn into the parking lot. My mother squeezed my arm, gently popped open the driver's side door, and slipped out into the night.

The minivan flicked off its lights and ground to a clattering halt in front of the curb. The side door wrenched open and three GFAs piled out. There were two men carrying rolled paper cylinders, and a

animal, or maybe a dead person. When one of the GFAs finally did pry up the floor panel, a cloud of insects burst up into her face, and she passed out, overwhelmed by the sight of something even more horrific than doll parts splashed in blood.

She climbed into the passenger seat, and I switched the car into neutral. I guided us back along the side of the building, and around to the opposite face of the clinic, where a twelve-foot chain-link fence bordered the slope down to the interstate.

We hugged, and I felt she was soaked through, and shivering. For fifteen minutes or so we just sat there, intermittently snickering in the dark.

Her cell phone vibrated and she answered. It was Charlie Birdsong; she'd had him stationed on the lookout in case anything went wrong.

Charlie reported that the GFAs were gone. Mom offered to give him a ride, but he wanted to stay and finish reading *Glamour*, then go to work on the new dead baby poster. My mother told Charlie not to stay up all night doing it, just to try and scrape the gooey head part of the fetus off. "Affirmative," I heard Charlie say. "It's definitely the gooey head that puts people off the most."

Emma let me pilot us out to the main road. We didn't talk. She rolled down the windows and the car filled up with sweet night smells, oak and wet lawns.

At a stop sign, I put the car into park. My mother had picked up the legal pad.

Why didn't you marry Dale?

She looked at me, a crease in her forehead. Emma licked her lips, as if she were about to speak.

I tapped the dashboard and shook my head. No talking. Not yet.

She jotted on the pad and held it up for me. *It's funny you should bring that up. We actually just got invited to Dale's wedding. And how much would Dale have loved this little escapade, by the way?*

I briefly gazed out the window. Outside, and running perpendicular to our parked car, a bus blurred past, the lit console and rows of darkened windows, maybe just arriving, maybe just leaving.

My mother wrote more: *He's marrying Gail Dahl, the art teacher from the high school. You had her last year, right? Mrs. Dahl? I guess she'll be Mrs. Crispin now, huh?*

I reached out and put my finger on the original question. I didn't know what I wanted to hear, but it suddenly seemed tremendously important.

In the harsh light of the roadside stanchions my mother no longer appeared so young. The streak of silver hair shone like it was polished. She grimaced, tapped the pen against her chin. She wrote, *I didn't think we were ready.*

I stared at the words. I took the pen. I underlined one word: *we*. She nodded at me.

I climbed out of the car and started to walk home.

But Emma refused to leave me; it was well past midnight and, after all, she was my mother. The car ground along just ahead of me, clinging to the shoulder, while I walked behind the trunk. I watched her headlights bob in the eaves of the roadside trees and wished to disappear, to wink out like an ember. I wished for her last glimpse of me to be in the rearview mirror, and for the rest of her life to be spent wondering what happened, what made me burn away. A dozen or so mosquitoes took up orbit around my head, but I refused to get back in the car.

Before we turned onto Route 12 and the final stretch to the house, I walked over to the all-night Citgo to seek a respite from the mosquitoes. My mother parked out front.

I bought an orange soda and the Goth cashier with the fork tattooed on his Adam's apple rang me up. "Dammit. Janet." With his purple-ringed eyes, he stared at me in stoned expectation.

"What?" I asked. "I just want a soda."

"I thought you rolled with the sex geezers?" He scratched his fork. "They don't take you to the movies, little hombre?"

"A soda," I said. I slapped a dollar on the counter.

"Dammit," he said, and took the dollar. "Janet."

I pushed out into the night and Emma wheeled around, taking the point down Route 12. By the time we reached the driveway, my feet ached, and my bare calves pulsed with bites. When she left the car, my mother didn't spare a backward glance, just clicked the electronic alarm, and walked inside. The only reason I didn't end the protest there and then, and start screaming at her, was that I was too tired.

A few minutes later, my body found its way into bed. I was asleep even before they started to fight.

8.

The next morning Dr. Vic stopped me when I called the Laddies to come for a walk. "I already took them out, George," he said. He was at the table, hunched over his morning crossword. "Come to think of it, I guess that's the way we might as well run it for the time being. It's good for me, taking them out. I need the exercise."

"Whatever you want, Doc." I pulled my house keys off the hook by the door.

"There's that damn woman again," he said, under his breath, jotting *Yoko* or *Ono* into his puzzle. Dr. Vic tossed down his pencil and his crossword book, and stood up with a screech of chair legs. "Let me give you a ride over to your grandfather's. We need to talk."

"I don't talk to strange men," I said.

On Route 12, the BMW pulled onto the shoulder and up beside me. He slowed down and unrolled the window. "Are you sure you don't want a ride?"

"I don't accept—"

Dr. Vic swung the BMW back into the road, turning up a spray of gravel.

But when I reached the house on Dundee Avenue, I found Dr. Vic already there; he was on the front lawn, helping Papa add a beard to Al Gore. Dr. Vic acted as though nothing had happened, just gave me a "howdy," and went on talking with Papa. My grandfather stood on a milk crate, using a Magic Marker to meticulously dab in the former vice-president's much discussed new whiskers. Some pundits had wondered if it was a statement of some kind, further evidence of the man's unbearable liberal pretension.

"They can't even let the man groom himself in peace," said Papa. "So he's not shaving. He's probably depressed. He's got a right to be. It's not enough they stole the election, now they're after the man's dignity, too."

Dr. Vic stayed on the ground and kept a hand on the other man's belt to make sure he didn't fall. "So let me get this straight, before the little bugger started vandalizing your sign, he stole your Travel section?"

I sat down on the hood of the Buick and crossed my arms.

"That was the start of it."

Dr. Vic shook his head. "What kind of a kid wants the Travel section of the Sunday *New York Times*? It's all stories about places you'll never go or, even worse, places you've been to, but that the article ends up making you feel guilty about because you missed all the really great stuff that stupid tourists don't know about."

Papa paused to extract a crumpled magazine page from his pocket and consult a picture of the former vice-president with his new beard. "He looks dignified, I think."

"I'll tell you, though, Henry, if you look on the bright side, at least the kid saved you the trouble of throwing it out."

"He took the Style section, too," said Papa. His voice contained an edge. He was shading in around Gore's cheeks, filling out the last few inches of gristle.

"Well," said Dr. Vic, "I suppose I can see how that might rile a man."

After Papa finished, he braced himself on Dr. Vic's shoulder and stepped off the crate. He gave a tiny groan when his shoes hit the grass and his weight came down. Dr. Vic asked him if he was okay. "Fine," said Papa, and shrugged off the other man's hand.

We all walked out into the street and surveyed the billboard:

Albert Gore Jr. won the 2000 election by 537,179 votes, but lost the presidency by 1 vote. DISGRACE. The leader of the free world is now a man who went AWOL from his National Guard unit, a huckster of fraudulent securities, a white-knuckle alcoholic, and a gleeful executor of the mentally handicapped. CRIMINAL. Our nation is in the midst of a coup d'état, perpetrated by a right-wing cadre that destroys the environment in the name of prosperity, hoards in the name of fairness, intimidates the voices of its critics in the name of patriotism, and wraps itself in the word of God. FARCE.

And below that the adjusted portrait of Gore, underscored by the legend:

THE REAL PRESIDENT OF THE UNITED STATES.

Below the text, Gore, and his beard, fixed south.

Papa held up the crumpled magazine page with the up-to-date picture of Gore, and we all looked back and forth between the two. The rendering was, I thought, quite accurate:

The former vice-president's facial hair appeared soft, almost tentative, hinting at curls if it were allowed to grow long enough. It was a beard that belonged to a much younger man, and it gave Al Gore's expression a morose quality, as if he were staring at the road for a ride that was late in coming, or more likely, never coming at all.

"You got him," said Dr. Vic.

Papa folded up the magazine page, and went over to the billboard. He took a rag out of his pocket and gave a quick polish to the union bug in the corner that marked it as the work of the printer in Providence.

"Even better," said Dr. Vic.

"Ayuh," said Papa. He rummaged in another pocket for a handful of peanuts, and started to crunch.

"Say, you should take it easy with those things, Henry. Not too many and not too fast, as they say."

"I don't want to hold you any longer, Dr. Lipscomb." Papa walked over to the BMW parked at the curb. I hopped off the hood of the car and followed him. "Be sure and tell Emma I said hello."

My grandfather gave me a wry glance, and added, "Or write it to her. Or do whatever it is you people do to communicate with one another these days."

"Will do," said Dr. Vic.

Papa held the door of the BMW open for his prospective son-in-law.

If he felt rushed, Dr. Vic didn't show it. After he shook my grandfather's hand and climbed into the car, he took his time feeling around for the keys. "And you'll give my best to Gil?"

"Very well, Dr. Lipscomb."

Dr. Vic didn't look up as he patted his breast pocket. "Who's his doctor, anyway? And how's he feeling? Emma told me that it was her impression that it was—pretty serious."

"I don't know. You'd have to ask Gilbert. But I guess he's hanging in there the best he can."

"Of course he is," said Dr. Vic. "Of course he is."

Bending his tall, lean frame at the waist, my grandfather reached through the car window, and poked the car keys. They jingled from the visor. The fob was a plastic cartoon Pekingese, wearing shades and riding a surfboard. "There."

"Ah." Dr. Vic snapped his fingers. He stuck the key in the ignition. He gave Papa a big smile and sat with his hand still on the head of the key. "I've got to ask: you feeling okay, Henry? You seem—I don't know. A tad frazzled."

The old man sighed. He jammed a hand in his trouser pocket and grabbed more peanuts. A few nuts popped out and went rolling crazily across the pavement.

"I'm fine," said Papa, and tossed back the peanuts. He started to chomp, talking between bites and breaths. "Mind you, our country is being run by a man who would just as soon wipe his ass with the Constitution as read it—and my First Amendment right is being trampled on by a member of the local chapter of the Hitler Youth—and everyone around here just walks around like they're deaf, dumb, and blind." He swept out his arms to indicate the scope of the catastrophe. A peanut fragment wobbled at the corner of his mouth. "Other than all that, Dr. Lipscomb, everything is fine. Everything is super."

Calm, and still holding the older man's gaze, Dr. Vic nodded. "And you lost your wife, Henry."

"That's right," said Papa. "I did lose my wife."

"Have you ever considered seeing a grief counselor?"

"Did you vote for Bush?"

"No."

"Did you consider it?"

"Yes."

My grandfather nodded. "No."

Dr. Vic raised an eyebrow.

"No, I never considered it. Going to a counselor. For my grief."

"I know a good one," said Dr. Vic.

They smiled at each other for a few seconds, the kind of squinting smiles that men use when they aren't really happy.

Dr. Vic turned the key and the engine awoke in a whoosh of high air-conditioning. "I'm going to have to insist that you start calling me Vic."

"Very well," said Papa. "Vic." He gave the BMW a rap on the roof.

Dr. Vic pressed the automatic window button and said, "I'm picking you up at four, George." He gave me a tight grin from behind the glass and backed up his car.

When the BMW disappeared around the curve in the road, Papa put his hand on my shoulder. It closed like a claw; I could feel him shaking. "I need to sit down."

We crouched down together. He hung on to my shoulder, lowering his rear, and then dropping the last couple of inches with a groan. I sat down beside him.

The pavement was warm from the sun. He breathed and clasped his hands in his lap. I reached out, flicked away the peanut at the corner of his mouth. He nodded, rocking a little, his breath hitching. Seconds passed, minutes. A car drove by, another car, a truck, cars and trucks.

I thought my grandfather might be about to cry. I had no idea what I would do if that happened.

"I've never sat in the driveway before," I said.

"I guess it's one of those places you don't usually sit."

His voice was tired, but controlled. Papa scanned around, taking in the lawn, the sign, the diminishing, ground-level viewpoint of the tall white house. "Well. Now you can check it off the List."

"The List?"

"The old Things-I-Did-Before-I-Died List."

"You, too," I said.

"Me, too," he said. A thoughtful, faraway expression came over his face. "You know who I bet has a hell of a list?"

"Who?"

Papa gestured in the direction of the Desjardins' house. "Gilbert."

"Really?"

"He's a hedonist."

"What's that?" I asked.

My grandfather grinned. "Better you don't know." He started to laugh—and then abruptly, his eyes grew wet and he stopped. He coughed several times and rubbed at his eyes. "Don't look," he said, and I closed my eyes while he blew his nose on the pavement.

When we were inside, making our way up the stairs, he leaned on me again, digging into my shoulder with his fingers. At the landing we stopped to rest. I could feel the vibration of his breath in my chest.

The previous autumn my freshman biology teacher, Mr. Capers, a spindly and excitable graduate student on loan from USM, had achieved some minor renown for raising a tarantula named Boris in the class aquarium. We marveled with repulsion at the creature's hairy, scuttling hunger, the way it devoured dead bugs and ravaged the papery fly corpses. Six classes worth of feedings, however, caused Boris to swell to the size of a fist, and he went belly-up over Christmas break. For the edification of future biology students, Mr. Capers, instead of disposing with the spider's body, installed Boris in a block of Lucite to use as a paperweight. But there must have been a breach in the paperweight's seal. Moisture soon appeared on the surface of the Lucite and one day, Boris's legs broke off. After that, the tarantula's body fell completely to pieces and rattled from one side to the other when you turned the paperweight over. Mr. Capers, soured by a full year of dealing with adolescents, began to patrol the class while holding the Lucite block of loose tarantula parts, and, if he saw a kid who wasn't paying attention, he would shake it aggressively at them.

The hard little tips of Papa's fingers brought up the memory of the tarantula in the Lucite block, all broken into pieces, the legs like matchsticks.

"Maybe you should see the doctor," I said.

"Just a little spell," Papa said. He let go of my shoulder, straightened, and walked the rest of the way without stopping.

I trailed him into the guest room. He sat in the chair by the orange-curtained window. "You know, sitting here, sometimes I feel like that bastard Oswald." One of his hands flopped in his lap. He squeezed it. "Don't worry. It was just a little spell, George."

For the first time, it occurred to me that if he wanted to, Steven Sugar could kill my grandfather, really kill him. If he had a grip on Papa, Steven Sugar could break the old man. I could see him doing it, could see him snapping my grandfather over one knee. I remembered how when Mr. Capers's Lucite paperweight was tilted, all the parts of the tarantula would pile up on one side like a mess of tiny blackened kindling.

I decided to tell Papa what happened at the library.

When I was done, he gave a grunt of satisfaction. "We're getting to him," he said.

I asked if we should call the police.

" 'My own private Vietnam'? He said that?" Papa peeled back the orange curtain and peered out at the sign. "Well, well, who's the sore loser now?"

"What about the police?" I asked again.

"What about them?" Papa held up his hand and flexed it a couple of times. Everything seemed to be under control.

"He said he would burn down your house."

My grandfather laughed. "I've heard that one before." He shot a finger pistol at the photograph of Joseph Hillstrom. "Isn't that what they always say, Joe?"

*   *   *

A few minutes later, he was asleep, one hand on the IL-47. I draped a blanket over him. Papa's hand stayed certain on the oiled wood of the grip.

When I went downstairs, I found Gil watching television and building a garbage joint from the buds in the ashtray. "Pull up a rock, lad. You know what time it is?"

I looked at the clock on the wall. "Noon?"

Gil crumbled a cinder into his paper. "Nope. It's Bare Ass O'Clock."

That was all the invitation I needed. I took a seat in Papa's armchair.

Gil had let himself in to see his favorite channel, an obscure cable station at the end of the dial that showed almost nothing besides an import about the lifestyles of naked Europeans, called *Bare Over There*.

In the months after Nana died and Gil's cancer was diagnosed, I often joined the two old men while they smoked up and vegetated for marathon sessions of *Bare Over There*. The three of us had been virtually hypnotized by astonishing wonders like the story of a pastry shop in a suburb of Zagreb where the topless waitresses served breast-shaped pastries, or the segment on the popular and controversial Latvian garage band who performed wearing nothing except Lincoln beards, and then fellated each other at the end of each show while simultaneously playing a (remarkably credible) cover of "Won't Get Fooled Again." We had seen other episodes about naked Spanish farmers who were tanned to the color of photo negatives, a naked mayor in Finland who married other naked people, and a benevolent cult of do-gooding nudists who rode the tram in Vaduz, offering to help old people carry heavy things. All over the world it seemed, people were living and working unrestricted by garments.

This afternoon's first episode concerned a nude circus troupe traveling through Spain.

"George?" Gil held up the glowing garbage joint. He stuck his hand under his arm and squeezed off a juicy fart. He winked at me. "When you get to college, you'll be glad that you did."

The mention of college put me in mind of pretty, pliant-breasted,

red-haired Myrna Carp of Vassar College, and how the pill had
saved her from having to kill anyone, how she planted that kiss on
my forehead. At Vassar College, I supposed, weed was common-
place. I also considered how much it would piss off my mother. Weed
was where it always started, and where Ty had started, too.

"What the fuck," I said.

"That's the spirit," said Gil.

He watched me draw a couple of hacking inhalations before
plucking the spliff from between my fingers. "Take a toke," said
Gil, giggling, "but don't choke."

I nursed a stone hard-on through the raven-haired looserope
walker's gymnastics, then grew nauseated by the performance of the
clown, a spidery-limbed creature whose balls were painted red, and
whose best trick was to pull miniature dildos from the hair of women
seated at ringside. On the couch, Gil watched through a pall of smoke.

I started to feel nervous, sweaty; I was aware of the hair on my
forearms and the old man's croaking laughs seemed to resound
within my head.

"Just about makes you want to drop everything, run away and join
the circus, doesn't it?" The smoke seemed to cling to Gil's skull, the
way fog hovered over a marsh in a scary movie.

"No," I said. "The clown is fucked up."

"You think he looks like Nader? The clown, I mean."

"What?"

"Ralph Nader," said Gil. "Try and picture the man with no clothes
on."

"I don't want to," I said. Ralph Nader was the furthest thing from
my mind. "Ever." Now my face felt tired. On the television the clown
was involved in a comical chase with a lion that was dressed in a lion-
sized pair of panties.

"I think there's a real resemblance," said Gil.

I nodded off for a couple of minutes, woke up for a second when
Gil shut off the television and walked out, then fell completely asleep.
I had a dream about my mother. We were at the table again, passing
our notebooks back and forth, as if we were having a conversation,
but our pens were charged with invisible ink. We cackled like mad

people. We threw paper everywhere. I went to a rally in front of my grandfather's house. Ralph Nader was on the stage, at the podium. He began to speak, his voice grave, his face graver, his skin hanging loose and masklike. "My Fellow Americans . . . I have gathered you here because our democracy has devolved into a single party system operated at the behest of a few monstrous corporations." He paused for effect. "I brought you here because my balls are painted red." I dreamt about riding my bike. I wove through miles and miles of road jammed with station wagon taxis.

My head ached and the clock said it was almost four. I went to the kitchen to find something to eat. The refrigerator, however, contained only V8 and condiments. In the cabinets I found several half-eaten jars of peanuts, and a few packets of bouillon.

Through the window over the sink, I could see the pool. Gil lay asleep, drifting nude on a purple inflatable recliner. A dictionary was open on his crotch, but the dark head of his penis poked, molelike, out from under the shelter of the pages.

"Jesus Christ," I said out loud, and hurried to be on my way.

9.

At the foot of Dundee Avenue I parked my bike behind a hedge and finished off a jar of peanuts. When I saw Dr. Vic's BMW drive past and around the curve, I remounted and started home the long way, looping around town to the south. Near the town line, without giving it much thought, I took a further detour, and swung into the development where Dale lived.

All of the houses here had been cranked out of the same mold, nondescript ramblers painted either white or sky blue, spaced out along a series of sweeping lanes that I supposed were meant to make the development seem less prefabricated and more like a village, but which instead gave the neighborhood a disorienting, House of Mirrors quality. It had been a while, and I got lost. Around every bend, I immediately recognized every house, only to realize a moment later that it was all slightly different—or maybe it wasn't, and I'd just come around in a circle. I remembered staying up late one night and watching a remake of *The Invasion of the Body Snatchers*. It was only later that I started to puzzle over the ramifications of the story; what happened when we were all gone, when we were all Pod People? I mean, what came next? I guessed maybe the Pod People would try to live like us, but not exactly know how, and they would end up building developments like this one where Dale lived, everything exactly the same, because that was what they thought it was like to be human.

When I finally did find Dale's house it was because of the black cat silhouette in the garage door window. I had been with him when he taped it up a couple of Halloweens ago.

The plastic kiddie pool in the front yard was new, though. As hot as it had been lately, I figured that Mrs. Dahl's kids must have loved to splash around in it. The driveway was empty.

I bet they played catch out here, Dale and the kids, the way we used to. That was last summer. When we played catch Dale opened up the front windows and jacked up the sound on the television so we could hear the ballgame at the same time. Cooking lunch, my mother liked to wheel the grill out into the driveway and watch us.

I fished a SpongeBob SquarePants figure out of the pool and twisted the legs off. I tossed the pieces in the grass, and immediately felt sorry. I went back, picked up the legs and the grinning sponge-shaped body. The toy's florid torso looked like a sad wreck to me, sadder still for the expression of happiness on the face, but I guessed some kid probably loved it.

I jammed the legs into their slots and made it a whole again. I set the toy on the rim of the kiddie pool so it looked like it was sort of hanging out, sunbathing or something.

Maybe Dale bought the kid the toy. Maybe he wrote the kid classifieds about it:

New Life: Sea Creature Sought
Sea crture needed fr wndrful new life. Must be lovble, squishy, bzzre. Excllnt kid, othr toys, hot mom, req.

Going home now felt like some kind of defeat, like admitting something—what I didn't know. I biked to the airport.

I sat at the fence in the shade of a wind-stripped oak tree, and watched the commuter planes and private jets land. On approach, they descended from the south, always skimming over the interstate at the same place, seeming to follow an invisible corridor, and sliding down the runway as easily as an arm pulling through a sleeve.

These planes were filled with summer people, vacationers from Connecticut and New York, heading to Kennebunkport and Cape Elizabeth for the weekend, to fish and Jet Ski and drop soda cans on the ground. For a week or ten days they would drink and piss in the lakes and buy grotesquely overpriced antiques and eat lobster until their plastic bibs were streaked with butter and flecks of white meat, before finally piling back onto another plane, aching and sunburned and eager to get back to civilization.

When we lived in Blue Hill my mother's ex-boyfriend Paul Bagley had supported his pottery studio by teaching tourists—and more often than not their bored, cunning children—how to mold and fire their own souvenir coffee cups and knickknacks. By nature, Paul was an almost supernaturally mellow man, whose own artistic creations typically represented a tiny man in a posture of repose, or else a bulbous fish of some kind, sporting a great, sorrowful mustache. That is to say, his sculpture was like himself: inoffensive, prone to very long naps, a little sad, and heavily whiskered. In the bi-yearly mayoral elections Paul dutifully stood for the Green Party, in 1994 garnering a mere twelve votes—which didn't include himself, because he forgot to vote.

But even Paul—soporific and uncritical Paul, who had seen the Grateful Dead two hundred and thirty-one times and swore that every single show was uniquely great—openly loathed the summer people who gave him his living. "Every year they show up and wreck the place," he said to me one night as I helped him sweep up. "They mess up my kilns and they mess up my supplies. Their kids mess up my john. I mean, put up the seat, right? Is that so hard? You put up the seat, right, George?

"Of course you do, but with these people, it's a whole different deal. After they're through, it's like it must have been after Altamont, like after some Downeast Altamont, except in my studio, you know. Broken shit all over the place."

"Do they even pay?" I asked.

"Sure, they pay," said Paul. He stooped to dig at a chunk of sneaker-printed saltwater taffy. "They always pay. That's the worst part. They think they can pay for anything. They think everything's got a cash value."

I watched a Learjet touch down in a whine of rubber and steam. When it pulled around to the terminal, a family of five crowded out. They were all heavyset and dressed in bright shorts and Hawaiian shirts. The son of the family, his torso like a stack of ice cream scoops under his flapping yellow shirt, jerked along a cocker spaniel on a leash and chugged from a two-liter bottle of soda. The spaniel yapped and squirted piss on the tarmac. Hurrying behind the family came the pilots of the jet, each of them bearing one side of an enormous steamer trunk, their ties snapping up in the breeze and whipping their faces.

A few moments after they disappeared into the terminal, the pilots jogged back out to the plane to retrieve the rest of the luggage.

The heavyset family was clearly rich, which meant they were probably conservatives—probably Republicans—which meant that in some deep and essential way, they either didn't care about anyone but themselves, or else believed that common decency was a risk they couldn't afford.

When the summer people went home to their high-rises, and their children returned to their private schools, I envisioned their daily lives as models for selfishness: I saw their route to work, and knew they drove miles out of their way simply to avoid the section of the city where black people shot each other. (That I had in my entire life known perhaps three African-Americans did not, of course, limit my judgement.) I could see the summer people as they went to church in their Mercedes, and I eavesdropped on their silent prayers and heard as they begged Jesus for lower taxes. (That I had, only a few days earlier, lain in bed and asked God not only to help me find evidence that Dr. Vic had committed a murder, but also to bring me a new fishing rod, seemed irrelevant.) I watched as they nodded at the priest's pronouncement that abortion was a mortal sin, and I waited to see no one stand up and ask, "Then what do we do with all the extra children? Who pays?" (Although I was one of these extra children, the kind that my mother could easily have aborted, I felt no debt to the Christians. After all, I wasn't extra now.)

Perhaps this kind of thinking wasn't so different from the way some people took comfort in the belief that affirmative action was the reason they couldn't find a job, and welfare was the reason they couldn't afford to take their children to the dentist. It threw up a great, thick sheet of tinted glass, and from behind it, I could make faces at passersby, and scream dirty words, and feel safe.

The reason I could see into the lives of the summer people so clearly was the same reason that my grandfather could see what a great president Al Gore would have been: because it had to be true.

I couldn't worry about exceptions. It was what they represented as a whole, the way they did what they wanted, and didn't bother with what anyone else thought, let alone how they voted. I may have been only fifteen years old, and only four years down the trail from a wholehearted belief in Santa Claus, but I could see that this wasn't about Al Gore. I could see that Albert Gore Jr., and a man like Henry McGlaughlin—who knew the words of the "Internationale" and relished them so well that he referred to it as a "hymn," and wanted it to be sung at his grave—were not exactly ideological soul mates.

It wasn't Al Gore that Steven Sugar wrote dirty words all over; it was my grandfather's identity, it was his home.

A home sometimes fell into disrepair: the paint peeled, the porch rotted, doorways grew crooked. People who lived in the place died. And, yet, this place was still home, and still held the memories of home, like a dusty jar, sealed tight with last winter's preserves. For my grandfather, there was no time to build a new one.

"So what's your excuse?"

For a moment my voice shocked me into silence. I stood with my fingers laced through the fence, staring at the parked Learjet. The runways were clear, the sky empty, the pine trees at the edge of the field tipped with brown.

"Fuck you," I told myself.

The family of pear-shaped, brightly clothed summer people emerged from the terminal with their luggage train. The fat boy yanked his dog's leash; the dog humped the leg of a porter.

They loaded the trunk of the first taxi at the curb, one of the local fleet of battered station wagons, and piled inside. The door of the taxi slammed shut with a creak of metal and a whine of rust. The cab belched away from the cement island. I slipped behind a tree, and scooted close to the bole, not wanting to be seen.

A few minutes later, Dr. Vic's BMW came around the parking loop. He honked and released the trunk. I waited for a couple of minutes, but he just sat in the front seat, tapping his fingers lightly on the wheel and looking straight ahead.

"I don't accept rides from strange men," I said.

"George, get in the damn car, would you? It's air-conditioned."

I tossed my bike in the trunk and climbed inside.

"Hey, you want a peppermint?" Dr. Vic shifted over to dig around in his pocket. He pulled out a broken dog biscuit, gave a grunt and felt around some more before producing a hard candy. Dr. Vic held it out; his grimace was sympathetic.

I stared at the mint.

"So be it." He unwrapped the peppermint and tossed it in his mouth.

We slid away from the curb.

"How did you know to come find me at the airport?" I asked.

Dr. Vic shrugged. "I figured you might have gone to see—" but he was wrong.

"You're wrong," I told him.

10.

The woods around the house were growing dusky by the time we returned to the house by the lake, but there still remained a couple of hours of good light. Dr. Vic told me there was something he wanted to show me. "There's something I want to show you, too," I said.

"Okay, that's super," he said, so eager that I almost felt sorry for him.

He told me to give him a second, and when he returned from the house he was accompanied by his Pekinese. At this sight, the minuscule insect of sympathy that had just hatched within my heart and was only beginning to take its first tentative steps, gave a brief spasm, and wilted to a husk.

Dr. Vic started for the woods, the dogs bolting out in front of him. I climbed onto my bike and pedaled behind.

He turned at the squeak of my gears. Dr. Vic clicked his tongue and gave his bald spot a dubious scratch. This was the absolute extent of his temper. "I thought we were going to walk."

"I prefer to ride," I said.

"All righty," said Dr. Vic.

We moved away from the house along the footpath that looped around Lake Keynes, passing under the spruce eaves and between the white stilts of birch trees. Around us the ground cover was lush with bursts of fern and checkerberry. The Laddies strained and whined and pitched their weight against Dr. Vic's double leash, like frantic little mops. I rode standing up, stoically grinding out the hard-packed bumps in the path. Odd chips of light, flashing off the lake, shot through the gaps in the foliage. There was a faint scent of char.

"They don't know they're small, do they?" Dr. Vic staggered after them, swiveling awkwardly to smile at me.

"They don't know anything," I said.

"Maybe so," said Dr. Vic, as always, ambushed by my dislike.

After about a half mile the footpath broke and we followed the split to the right, away from the lake and toward the hills.

"How's your granddad?" Dr. Vic talked to me now without looking back.

"He's all right."

"Sounds like this Sugar kid is a real little punk."

"Papa says he's just your basic, garden-variety fascist."

"Maybe so."

We walked a bit farther.

"What are you two fellas up to over there every day, George?" Dr. Vic held back a branch and looked straight at me. A small frown played across his mouth.

"Nothing," I said, and slipped by, then pulled up and waited for him to go ahead again. He let the long black branch snap back. "Horseshit," said Dr. Vic.

"What do you mean?"

"You're up to something."

"Whatever." Again, I caught a whiff of the burnt smell, like old charcoal.

"And I don't suppose you'll care to shed any more light than your mother did, about what you and she were doing last night?"

"You suppose right."

"Listen, George. I agree with everything he put on that sign. Al Gore got a stiff one in the backdoor, and not so much as the courtesy of a wraparound." He coughed. "I'd appreciate it if you didn't tell your mother I put it just that way, but you know what I mean."

"Sure," I said. "I won't tell her that you think Al Gore got fucked up the ass."

Dr. Vic exhaled.

After a few seconds, though, he went on: "Still, at the same time, it's not like they put Adolf Hitler in the White House. Look, Bush might not be the worst thing that's ever happened. He seems like a decent enough guy. I mean, he's a lot of things, but he's not, like your granddad would say, 'a garden-variety fascist.' He's just a good old boy. The country'll survive."

Dr. Vic stopped to pick up the Laddies. They squawked and slobbered with pleasure. In the manner of a commuter with a rolled up newspaper, he neatly stuck one sausage-shaped dog under each arm, and ported them as he squatted to climb under a low, heavy branch. I dismounted and left my bike propped against a tree.

"So whatever it is you two are up to, you better have some sense about it. And it better not be dangerous."

I crawled under the branch. "Or what?"

There was a muddy dip in the path. The Laddies immediately scrambled into the mud and began to wrestle and yip. Dr. Vic pointed to a mossy log in the brush. He took one end and I took the other. We set it across the dip and strolled across. He poked the dogs with a branch; they raced ahead, knowing the way, whipping through the underbrush.

"Well?" I asked. "Or what?"

"Does your grandfather blame me for Gerry dying, too?"

They had barely been able to squeeze Nana's full name onto her headstone: *Geraldine Sarah Niven McGlaughlin.* Her epitaph had read: *Wife, Mother, Worker, "Don't Mourn! Organize!" 1928–2000.*

"No, he doesn't. I don't blame you, either. That's just something I told Mom to make her feel bad."

He tramped a few more yards before responding. "I'm glad. I like your grandfather. I like you, George." I heard the telltale click of his tongue. "I don't think you're a mean kid, either, but that's a nasty thing to say, even if you didn't mean it. Nasty to me, and to your mother. You can't do that."

"I can do anything I want," I said.

We made the last quarter mile in silence and emerged from the trees into a clearing that held the desiccated hulk of an old Studebaker truck. The ground beneath the vehicle had sunk, as if the Studebaker were gradually burying itself. A sapling grew up through the empty trunk and all that remained of the seats were the metal frames. Nearby, a pile of blackened stones and charred sticks marked a recent campfire.

"Neat, huh?"

"Sure," I said. "Neat."

The big man sat down on the Studebaker's running board and patted the space beside him. Pretending not to notice, I strolled over to the campfire and kicked a stone. I stuck my hand under my arm and squeezed off a few indiscreet pops, the way Gil had taught me.

Dr. Vic nodded. Dark patterns of sweat had formed at his armpits and at the crease of his belly, and again, I nearly found it possible to sympathize with him. He was a big man, soft and awkward, gone gray and losing what there was of that, his life held hostage by a fifteen-year-old boy. I guessed he was weary of it. Maybe I was, too.

"I came across this truck one time a couple of years ago. I was just wandering, you know? And, here's this amazing artifact, in what's really a very unlikely place. It really struck me, George, and I've given a lot of thought about how it got here.

"You see, the thing that stumped me is that the fire road's a mile away. So whoever drove through the woods had a rough go of it. Which means the truck must have been in pretty good shape."

The dogs lay down in a heap at his feet, panting happily. He rubbed their heads. "From that point, George, I can conceive of only three possible scenarios:

"First, that it was a bootlegger's truck. Some old gangster jack-knifed it right off the road, came barreling through here, dumped the wheels, the hooch, and headed for the hills."

The ghost of a rawboned country bootlegger, overalls and rubber boots and a pencil-thin mustache, ran through the underbrush in my mind, holding down his straw boater with one hand, and gripping a sawed-off shotgun in the other. He cast a desperate glance over his shoulder, and disappeared into a stand of white pine.

"You like that one, huh?" Dr. Vic grinned at me.

I shrugged, but couldn't restrain a little grin of my own.

"Okay, right. Now in my second scenario I have a guy—a husband, a father—and he lost it, totally lost it. Got completely fed up with everything, and said, 'Forget it all. My job, my wife, my kids, I don't give a good goddamn about anything, anymore. Forget the whole thing.' This guy, he drove the car real deep in here so no one would find it. Then, he walked out to the road, stuck a thumb, and never looked back."

In my mind I heard the dull, painful thud of a patent leather shoe striking a long-vanished hubcap, as the man who just didn't care but somehow that brought the argument closer, as if it were happening inside my own mind, and being fought between warring personalities. "And what the fuck are you doing sifting through my checkbook, I'd like to know?" asked Dr. Vic, finally gathering steam.

The matter of Dr. Vic having surreptitiously donated two hundred dollars to the presidential campaign of George W. Bush turned out to be only the starting-off point, for this raised questions about their entire relationship. My mother wanted to know if Dr. Vic had been leading her along from the very beginning, pretending to support her career at Planned Parenthood; and whether he was lying when he said he believed in a woman's right to choose. What about contraception? Did he realize that in the eyes of the man in the White House, the man he gave money to, that his fiancée was bound to burn in hell for the mortal sin of teaching teenagers how to use condoms? Did it concern a big-money Republican donor like himself that—and so on, and so forth, and even when I retreated to my bedroom, their voices chased me up through the windows and the floors, and with my head buried in a pillow, I begged them to stop.

I fell asleep for an hour and two, and woke to find the house quiet. My mother had slipped a note under the door. *I always told you that you could succeed at whatever you wanted. What you're doing now, what your grandfather is helping you to do—to Victor and me—is no exception. I wish I could be proud of you again. I don't know if your grandfather put you up to it, but it doesn't matter. I raised you better. I'm so ashamed of you both.*

The silence was only an intermission, however, and they started up again almost as soon as I finished reading. At the same time, the Laddies yelped and hurled themselves against the chain-link fence of the kennel, like rioting lunatics. My mother and Dr. Vic took their argument out to the dock now, where so recently they had drunk wine and danced and kissed and laughed about all the funny things you learned about someone when you fell in love with them. Their voices were now indiscernible, just sounds, Dr. Vic rumbling in protest, and my mother snapping back, every word like a whip being cracked. The barking and the yelling mixed with a series of splashes, but by then I couldn't even bear to raise up and see if they were drowning each other.

11.

I dreamt that I was stranded at the side of the road. The moon hung in the air like a porthole in the night, like an entrance to the day.

I started walking. A Studebaker taxi pulled past me, then ground up onto the shoulder. It kept on going, just staying in front of me, but I was tired of being left behind. I hurled a rock off the back window. The taxi crunched to a stop.

Myrna Carp pushed open the door and told me to come on. From the Bob Dylan album she was holding, she suggestively extracted a record-sized condom.

"I thought you were on the pill," I said.

"Just get in the damn taxi," she said.

I did.

12.

The cackle of a loon roused me at dawn. I went to look out the window.

The night sky had paled to a woolly gray, but the lake was still black, so the silver circles floating in the shallows by the dock were sharply defined. There were roughly three dozen of these flashing objects, drifting on the placid water like tiny, baffled UFOs.

I cracked the window to let in some air. I wiped my eyes with my fists and took a few deep breaths to clear away the last of the dreaming.

The silver circles were still there when I looked again, slowly rotating on the surface of the lake. The first ray of the sun shot over the hills on the southern end of the lake and burst across the circles in a single snap, like a giant flashbulb going off.

They were compact discs, I realized, all those silver circles. There was something mesmerizing in the sight, the way the little pieces of plastic filled with light. It didn't seem strange, only sad and pretty.

I worked it out, then, that there was only one person in our house who had a vast enough music collection to account for so many discs. From there it followed that when the argument proceeded onto the deck, the splashing I heard must have been the sound of my mother throwing her fiancé's maudlin CD collection into Lake Keynes.

This was a very humorous development, I decided, a final come-uppance for everything that made Dr. Vic, Dr. Vic. "It's a wonder the lake didn't spit them back," I pronounced, because the moment of victory was not the time for the hero to drop his cavalier attitude. Oddly enough, however, I found it impossible to produce the correct grin of satisfaction.

I reminded myself of the situation: there was a line, and it was our line, and you had to be very careful about what kind of person you let come across. Just as a union acted for mutual benefit, it was founded on mutual trust. It had never until now been more clear to me why I couldn't believe in Dr. Vic's commitment—what made him so different from the men my mother dated before, Paul and Jupps and Dale and the others, who had respected the line, and understood exactly how close they could toe up to it. What made Dr. Vic different was not his big, lumpy, ridiculous body, or his pockets full of dog biscuits and peppermints, or the corny scraps of poetry that he stuck on the fridge. What made him different was the cross-training, the same act that had made Tom Hellweg a blackleg. If he simply wanted to be my mother's husband, maybe that would have been okay, maybe we could have negotiated some kind of settlement. I could be reasonable. Except, Dr. Vic had been cross-training from the beginning: sitting me down to talk about life, taking me for a walk to discuss things—all the time, trying to be the man, the man of the house, the one who explained how things were and how the world worked, the man who gave me rides home.

That first blast of daylight clung to the silver discs and rimmed them with gold sparks. "It's a wonder the lake didn't spit them back," I repeated to myself, because it was just so funny.

*   *   *

Before leaving the house I paused at the door of the master bedroom and pressed my ear to the door. Dr. Vic's sound therapy machine was on, a soothing tide, low breakers falling and receding, but behind the gentle rush I could hear talking. The conversation was modulated now, almost hesitant, like a discussion of the weather in a beginners' language class. The argument was apparently over, although I didn't know what that could mean. I waited, scared and nervous and excited, but the soft tones did not lift and the small waves continued to lick at an invisible shore.

When I reached my grandparents', I found the two old men sitting in the living room with the air-conditioning on high, a fresh bowl smoldering, the television on mute, and the radio on the window-sill turned to the local talk station. Gil curled up on the couch in his pajamas, his naked head propped on a pillow. Papa slouched in the armchair, and the bowl rotated back and forth between them.

My grandfather glanced up at me with eyes slit to bloodshot quarters, and nodded. "Grandson," he said. "Comrade." He seemed to be searching for more words, but settled for another nod, and turned back to the television.

"You're just in time, lad," said Gil. "We've got bare-assed Swedes."

The show was muted so that my grandfather could listen to the radio at the same time.

I sat down on the floor. I felt relieved to be away from the house, relieved and safe and somehow more myself. I realized how tired I was then, how fitfully I must have slept while my mother and Dr. Vic yelled through the night. A part of me wanted to blurt out, "How could you?" and demand that my grandfather tell me why he called my mother and started the whole thing. Another part of me scolded this thought; wasn't that exactly what I wanted? Was I about to start doubting him now?

The old men coughed the bowl back and forth, the one dying, the one crazy, but the only people that I could really trust. In this place, I felt no doubt that we were all on the same side.

The purple bags beneath Papa's eyes were the size of butterfly wings. He must hardly have slept for weeks, sitting beside the window until dawn, with his rifle and scope, on the lookout for the vandal Steven Sugar.

"First thing in the morning I called an old hand I knew at the yards in Norfolk, and I asked him if he could clear a spot for a friend of the family who needed a change of scenery. Gerry made the offer, and the son-of-a-bitch Hellweg said he was amenable to the idea, but only on two conditions: First of all, he wasn't partial to traveling coach, since it cramped the leg he'd broken when he was a kid. Second of all, long trips gave him dry mouth.

"So, by that night we had them in a first-class car from Portland to Boston to Norfolk with a case of beer and a bottle of whiskey." My grandfather barked an abrupt laugh and broke into a series of deep, hacking coughs. He put the corner of the comforter up to his mouth and continued hacking for more than a minute. When the coughs passed, he continued in a whisper. "And the next I heard—the last I ever heard—my old friend Tom Hellweg was working as a riveter, pulling a pension and a family health insurance plan, double over-time and five weeks of vacation a year, just like any worker deserves. A living wage and some respect, what Gerry and I spent the better part of our lives fighting to get for our people."

I let out the breath I had been holding.

My grandfather looked down at the wet smear on the comforter. He touched it with the tip of his finger. "You understand that it was a moment of weakness, George," he said. "If Tom had his way, that could have been the daughters of any one of the hundred men at the Works who would have lost their jobs. You understand that, don't you? You understand that compassion will get you nowhere when you're dealing with a man who doesn't even have compassion for his own offspring?"

"Yes," I said, and Papa nodded and then he said a few more things, about the president's shameless pandering, about the unchecked corporations and the systematic dismantling of the Bill of Rights, about the obscenity of "compassionate conservatism" and about a lot of other things that were also true and which made people feel bad to even talk about. But they needed to talk about it, damn it. Staying quiet was the reason we were in so much trouble in the first place, and he, for one, wasn't going to shut up. He wasn't going to be picked on (**GET OVER IT!**), either, and he wasn't going to be intimidated (**LOVE IT OR LEAVE IT!**), and he certainly wasn't about to be libeled (**COMMUNIST!**), not by anyone, boy or man. No, no, no. Not at this late stage.

When he ran down, I tucked another blanket over him, and he shut his eyes and fell asleep. I sat down in the armchair by the window and took aim at the yard, at the blue plastic backing of the billboard, at the empty street. I woke up the same way, hunched over the rifle, the street still void of targets.

It was late afternoon when my grandfather came to. The wind had suddenly kicked up, blowing eddies of dust and cut grass down the street, and shivering the tree branches. The rush of air came in through the open window and rustled the orange curtains. Papa groaned and pulled himself upright.

"Thunderstorm," I said.

Papa rocked back and forth, slapping and rubbing his arms, as if he were cold, although it must have been eighty degrees in the upstairs room, and humid, too. "Gotta wake up, get the juices flowing," he said.

I offered to stay the night. He said that wasn't necessary. His eyelid twitched, and he plucked at it. "If you really wanted to help out an old man, though, I wouldn't protest if you went next door to see if Gil couldn't scare up a few spare herbs." Red blooms appeared on his arms where he slapped them.

"What do you think of Dr. Vic?" I asked. I had never spoken to my grandfather about the situation at home. I assumed that he and my mother had discussed it; but that he wanted to give me space to bring it up on my own.

Papa shrugged. "As a doctor, or as a son-in-law?"

"Both," I said.

"As a doctor, your grandmother liked him. That was what mattered to me. Lipscomb was honest, and to the point, and didn't make any promises he couldn't keep. She was terminal from the get-go and he told her straight. Lipscomb said he'd make her as comfortable as he could, and I believe he did that." Papa rubbed his thighs and clapped his hands. "As a son-in-law, he's a fat man, which is embarrassing in light of his profession. He's also too old for her, which means that it's likely that before all is said and done she'll have to be his nurse. Furthermore, he gave money to that sacrilegious son-of-a-bitch who stole the election, which was at the very least a failure of some kind of nerve, and a goddamned shame in general. And, of course, he's boring, which is a personal disappointment."

He reached out, then, his long, wrinkled finger hovering less than an inch in front of my face. The gesture froze me; I thought he was about to give me the finger, like Dr. Vic the night before; that he was about to accuse me of sulking, of cruelty to animals, of admiring Steven Sugar for his courage, of envying his capacity for destruction, of all these and many other crimes of which I was guilty. An apology filled my mouth. I nearly blurted out, "I'm not really like this. I want to fix this!"

Papa flicked a sleep seed from the corner of my eye. It was a gesture I remembered from when I was very small, when the hair at his temples was black. "But disappointment is no surprise. I've been disappointed on a regular basis since Congress passed the Taft-Hartley. Therefore, knowing what she knows now, if your mother insists on loving the man, then I will resign myself to having a closet Republican for a son-in-law. At least he's not a Yankees fan.

"I spent my life working under a system of collective bargaining. Collective bargaining is a synonym for disappointment. The act of collective bargaining is, essentially, the act of bilging a sinking ship that is beyond the reach of land or rescue. Although it's hopeless, you keep on doing it until you drown."

"Why?" I asked.

"Because only a crazy person lets themselves drown."

He smiled, a wide, strong, yellow smile—so strong and so hard a yellow that it looked like it could have slipped out of his mouth and fallen to the floor and not even chipped. I smelled his bad breath, the marijuana and the peanuts that were the only thing I ever saw him eat anymore.

I smiled back.

The old man reached out for the jar of peanuts on the bedside table, grabbed a handful.

"And while it's my opinion that workers deserve democracy, real democracy, I also believe that in life the best we can hope for is collective bargaining." My grandfather shrugged then, and said, "But I'm sure I don't have to tell you about that, George. If I recall, you've known some disappointment yourself."

Gil's wife ushered me into the Desjardins' house, a dainty brick structure that for me always recalled the story of the big bad wolf. The last piggie had inhabited just such a brick house, and no amount of wolfish huffing and puffing had managed to topple it. In her gingham apron and slippers, stout, middle-aged Mrs. Desjardins went nicely with the fairy tale theme.

"And just in time," she said as she led me into the living room, speaking with the sitcom brightness that was her typical tone. "Gilbert's being incorrigible again."

She was Gil's fourth or fifth wife, my grandmother had mentioned to me once, and like him, a former professor at the University of Southern Maine. "I think she taught literary theory," Nana said, never one to hide her skepticism, "which is bullshit, by the way." Although she was past fifty, Mrs. Desjardins was the sole person I knew who could be described—could *only* be described—as "chipper." At the reception following Nana's funeral she patrolled the living room with a garbage bag, briskly collecting paper plates as soon as they were cleared, and stuffing them away like hazardous medical waste.

I had never understood what Gil saw in her, but I assumed it related to being old and still wanting to have sex and making the best of a limited number of options. I tried not to think about it, though.

For his part, Gil always claimed that their relationship was largely based on Scrabble. I had heard him lecture on the subject several times as the marijuana smoke wavered about his head and Papa

ndians and shredding the purloined sections
and flinging the confetti in the air. He could
d I doubted my grandfather would so much

me coalesced into a frank realization: in my
suddenly diminished, and I felt diminished by
d somehow been allied. Here was an old man
e to shoot his enemies with a gun that wasn't
Sugar wasn't a fascist; he was just an asshole
rred to me with a kind of amazement. This
s pointless.

othing, I thought to myself. Why does Steven
d at Papa, slumped over, the thread of drool
nshaven chin. Why does *he* bother? It was like
rt, just because you could.

nothing," I said.

ight in the chair, rearranged his hands, and
os, I repeated these words aloud to my grand-
yond hearing.

14.

 Dr. Vic's house the sound of approaching
ith the slamming of windows against the com-
me feel as though I were being chased, but that I
vas ahead.

hat I needed to say to them. The breadth of the
d to make astonished me. I felt big and strong
o give them a chance. They would want to hug
 let them hug me. They would cry; and I was
nese movements were as plain and clear to me as
e far end of the rifle's scope, so clear and so plain
lish person might attempt to reach around and
tion with their fingers.

midity fell over my shoulders like a wool shawl.

looked on with a grimace. "The first time we played, she froze the board, got us all blocked into one corner, and then waited for me to get impatient. And when I finally got flustered and put down *cat*—it was the only thing I could do at that point and I just wanted to expand the board—she drops an *afalque* on the end and makes *catafalque*. Scored one hundred and sixteen points." Gil said that was when he knew. "I had wanted to fuck women all my life, George, but she made me think about the part that would come later, the part that would come when all the fucking was through. It was then that I foresaw I would need a challenging Scrabble competitor."

So when Mrs. Desjardins brought me into the living room I wasn't surprised to find the board was spread out on the table, and Gil hunched over in concentration. Behind him, the bow window gave onto the rapidly darkening afternoon; thunderclouds scuttled over the distant treetops. He was seated in the wheelchair that he used in the house and, oddly, there was a thin band strapped across his forehead, holding a hat or something to the back of his bare skull.

"You have a visitor, Gilbert. The boy's come to see if you might have any drugs that he can run over to his grandfather."

"Hey, Gil," I said.

Gil threw up a hand. "A moment, please, lad." He wore only an undershirt and a pair of blue boxer shorts, leaving his pale-haired, skinny legs and knobby knees exposed.

Mrs. Desjardins rolled her eyes at me. Over her shoulder, on the wall, hung an oversized Helmut Newton print of a towering nude in heels, her face half concealed by a leather bandit's mask, and the rest of her body concealed by nothing whatsoever. The photograph was taken from below and in front of the wrought iron gates of a castle. This angle emphasized the model's blond-haired pubis, and mini-mized the bartizan in the background, which appeared to grow up from her head like a horn.

"You see the symbolism?" asked Mrs. Desjardins. She had fol-lowed the direction of my gaze. Her bright, interested eyes reminded me of a seagull's eyes, the way it looked at a wrapper or a bit of foil lying on the ground—right before stabbing it.

"Yes," I said.

"Of course you do," said Gil. He spoke without removing his attention from his slate of letters. "These days I find that particular image rather discouraging. I'll leave the deduction to you, George."

The frame was slightly off, and Mrs. Desjardins adjusted it with a finger. "It's obvious, but that's the fun. I mean we're not talking about Immanuel Kant."

"You're embarrassing him," said Gil. "And for God's sake, leave Kant out of this."

"What I mean is we're not talking about rocket science. We're talking about the things that everyone does." Mrs. Desjardins gave me a shrug and a roll of the eyes. She mouthed the word "Grumpy."

I had an odd, uncomfortable feeling; a prickle that started in my stomach and moved up through my chest in waves. This was a sensation I associated with the time when I was small and my mother would go on dates. My grandmother, who often babysat on these occasions, could perceive my growing nervousness as the hours passed. "Stop twitching, Georgie darling. You look like someone just sang Irving Berlin over your grave. She'll be home soon." Now, looking back among the towering German nude, Mrs. Desjardins's too curious eyes, and Gil sitting at the table with whatever it was strapped to his head, I had that same sense of vague but insistent worry.

But in the next moment, the feeling dissipated. I realized that I didn't have time to be worried. I suddenly knew that I needed to go home and try to talk to them. I knew that it was time to apply the principles of collective bargaining.

"Papa said he just wanted a couple of buds if you could spare it. He's kind of worn out."

Gil clucked at his letters. "I sympathize. Believe me. It's going around."

This comment elicited a sigh from his wife.

I stood, resisting the urge to jump from foot to foot. I wasn't a bad kid. I wasn't Steven Sugar. I just wanted to make a point, to have my say. It was like the dream in the mall. If everyone would just slow down, slow down and stop and listen, then I could say what I had to say, and—

"The chi
"Fine," h
"Take a l
wheelchair,
the mask of
could see the
expression w
red bulb of a
and nodded
was thinking

Mrs. Desja
George. He d
me out,' he ca
contain a glim
and chuckled
thing, and nov

With a grun
it's a good ide
from the upsta
showed me hi
pinched a few

My grandfather
the window wit
spit unfurled fr
reeled back in
hands lay clench
balls into plasma
windowsill.

When I gave hi
like a stuffed anin
crumbs on the fr

If he wanted to
board, he could
portrait, then defe
a circle with his lie

of them whooping like
of the *New York Times*
do all that and more, a
as stir.

My need to rush ho
mind Steven Sugar was
association, as if we ha
in a window, desperat
even a real gun. Steven
kid. The thought occu
wasn't a fight; this wa

This accomplishes n
Sugar bother? I looke
now leaking over his u
taking something apa

"This accomplishes
As I lifted him stra
brushed off the crum
father, but he was be

On the ride back to
thunder alternated w
ing storm, and made
was winning, that I

I tried to think of
treaty I was prepare
lunged. I was going
me; I was willing to
willing to cry, too. T
the things I saw at th
that a child or a foo
touch the magnifica

The thickening hu

Garage doors began to jerk closed as I sped past, as if my wheels were tripping invisible wires.

I was drenched in sweat when I reached the driveway and jumped off my bike running, letting it crash in the grass. At the top of the porch, I looked back and noticed that the windows of Dr. Vic's BMW were down. My legs were pulsing, but I ran over anyway, and rolled them up tight.

As I stepped into the house, my yell caromed through the high, spacious rooms. "Hello? Hello? I'm back!"

I ran down the hall and threw open the door to the living room. "I'm back!" I yelled again, the words crossing my lips even as I saw that there was no one here either, just the drapes lapping in the open window, and a trapped fly buzzing around the suitcases lined up against the wall.

The fly circled and abruptly dropped down onto the handle of the first suitcase in the line, my mother's indestructible old Samsonite. The portmanteau's baby blue facing was dented from all the Greyhound luggage compartments that I had kicked it into, cracked from all the third-floor apartments whose stairs I had used it to sled, and patched so neatly with duct tape that it could almost pass for whimsical.

The careful tape job had always irritated me. I remembered watching as my mother sat on the floor of the apartment we rented in Boothbay, a dreary little box of a place stacked on top of a diner, where the stench of bacon rose up from below, continuously, with the substance of an awful, unceasing fart. Even at age eight, I was astounded by the sight of her crouched on the ochre-colored shag rug, wearing her pajamas and a pair of rhinestone sunglasses, as she went about the meticulous process of trimming off the strands at the end of each piece before laying them down like strips of papier-mâché. Did she actually believe there was any repair she could make to this thrift store luggage that would fool someone into thinking we actually belonged somewhere, that we had a house and a family to whom we were traveling home?

The sight of the suitcases made me uneasy. I told myself that Emma must have been preparing to throw some of our old things away, or maybe she was going to donate it all to the Goodwill store, which is where most of it had come from anyhow. Of course that was it. They were getting married; they must be expecting new luggage. Of course.

The insect jerked into the air again, fluttered hopelessly for a few seconds, and landed down on the last piece of luggage in the line, a black suitcase with a Lufthansa sticker on the side. My mother's ex-boyfriend Jupps Boger had left it behind when he flunked out of his graduate program and went to live in Norway, where his friends ran a hydroponic farm. "I love her, you know? She is a tough one, with the boy and the going to school," Jupps told me the last time I saw him. My mother had been in the airport drugstore, buying him a toothbrush and deodorant. "I am a fuck-up, you know, but less always since I know her." In his zipperless leather jacket with pink piping, my mother's ex-boyfriend hugged his backpack like a little boy and made a confession. "Your mother is very generous, though. Do you think, if I forgot my suitcase, she would bring it to me in Amsterdam?" He attempted a sly grin, but his eyes were wet. "I have completely forgot my suitcase in order only to remember it."

We never did hear from Jupps again, but we took his suitcase along with us everywhere we went, just in case. It was my favorite suitcase, because it was the lightest; the only things it contained were a couple of pairs of medium-sized black briefs, an empty pack of German cigarettes, and a yellowed *International Herald Tribune* from October 22, 1995, with half the crossword completed. We had a moving ritual, my mother and I, of loading everything into the car, and then taking a final walk through the empty rooms of our apartment. When we were certain we didn't leave anything, I would pick up Jupps's suitcase, and say, "Let's ride, Jupps," and my mother would lock the door behind us.

The rising wind slapped the drapes against the sill, and as I stood in the doorway I became aware of my own breathing. I had forgotten what it felt like to look at a line of luggage and know that our whole lives were inside.

Walking through the house, I paused at their bedroom, where my mother's closet had been cleared of everything but a few wire hangers. On the third floor, I found the door open, and the room neat and empty. The walls were naked except for a few holes in the plaster. The smart oak desk for which I had never thanked Dr. Vic was cleared. Fresh white sheets were on the bed; the ragged old quilt of peace symbols that Nana sewed for me was gone, too, packed up with everything else.

I found myself at the window. A bead of rain splashed on the glass, then another. A ripple of dots plinked across the surface of the lake.

The break in the weather, however, appeared to have no effect on Dr. Vic. My mother's fiancé stood at the end of dock, a highball in one hand and a dowel in the other, sipping serenely.

At the sound of my steps on the wood, he turned and squinted through his wet glasses. I stopped at the foot of the dock, but he lifted his dowel in greeting. "Hey, how's it going?"

I didn't know what to do. It wasn't supposed to be like this. I was ready to accept their apology. I was ready to come back to the bargaining table.

The rain had already gathered from a drizzle into a light, steady fall, and the shoulders of Dr. Vic's shirt were now dark.

There was a bench near him at the end of the dock, and I saw a carton of orange juice and a bottle of vodka sitting on it, along with a stack of the compact discs that he had fished out of the water so far. Beneath the bench, the Laddies crouched beside each other with their snouts resting on the planks, like a couple of vagrants huddled under a bridge.

Dr. Vic tossed back the dregs of his screwdriver. He raised the empty highball for me to see. Rain spattered in the glass. The wind was kicking up, sweeping the lake, cutting tiny waves.

"I need more ice!" he yelled.

I didn't understand. I yelled, "I put up the windows of your car, so the seats wouldn't get wet!"

Dr. Vic looked at me without any seeming comprehension.

I made a rolling gesture. "So that seats of your car wouldn't get wet!"

"I need more ice!" He smiled and gave the empty highball a demonstrative shake.

Now I understood, and it scared me a little.

"Where's my mother?"

Dr. Vic cocked his head. His smile widened. "She left me! Hopped on the first choo-choo to Splitsville!" Flourishing the dowel, he gave the empty highball a tap with the handle, the way a magician raps the brim of his top hat with a wand. "Abracadabra!" he hollered. "Stepped the fuck out! And now no ice!"

In the kitchen, I found my mother's note dashed on a piece of lined yellow paper, stuck to the fridge:

> *George, went to pick up apartment keys from the realtor. Back by six o'clock. Wait.*
>
>   *—Mom*

I was too late.

My gaze fell on the poem taped beside the note, one of Dr. Vic's old ones, inspired by the Fourth of July:

> *If She Were Tea (But She's Not Tea!)*
> *By Victor Lipscomb*
> *The beautiful fireworks blew up the sky*
> *The way a beautiful woman can blow up a lonely guy.*
> *If she were a box of tea*
> *I'd have to keep her with me.*
> *George Washington, see you later!*
> *If loving her makes me a traitor,*
>
> *I'd rather be a British.*

I took a tray of ice cubes from the freezer, found a raincoat, and returned to the dock. Dr. Vic was face down on the wood on his belly, as if he'd been shot in the back. I immediately knew that he had suffered a heart attack. He had had a heart attack and it was my fault. I had screwed up the life of a perfectly inoffensive man, looked on with a grimace. "The first time we played, she froze the board, got us all blocked into one corner, and then waited for me to get impatient. And when I finally got flustered and put down *cat*—it was the only thing I could do at that point and I just wanted to expand the board—she drops an *afalque* on the end and makes *catafalque*. Scored one hundred and sixteen points." Gil said that was when he knew. "I had wanted to fuck women all my life, George, but she made me think about the part that would come later, the part that would come when all the fucking was through. It was then that I foresaw I would need a challenging Scrabble competitor."

So when Mrs. Desjardins brought me into the living room I wasn't surprised to find the board was spread out on the table, and Gil hunched over in concentration. Behind him, the bow window gave onto the rapidly darkening afternoon; thunderclouds scuttled over the distant treetops. He was seated in the wheelchair that he used in the house and, oddly, there was a thin band strapped across his forehead, holding a hat or something to the back of his bare skull.

"You have a visitor, Gilbert. The boy's come to see if you might have any drugs that he can run over to his grandfather."

"Hey, Gil," I said.

Gil threw up a hand. "A moment, please, lad." He wore only an undershirt and a pair of blue boxer shorts, leaving his pale-haired, skinny legs and knobby knees exposed.

Mrs. Desjardins rolled her eyes at me. Over her shoulder, on the wall, hung an oversized Helmut Newton print of a towering nude in heels, her face half concealed by a leather bandit's mask, and the rest of her body concealed by nothing whatsoever. The photograph was taken from below and in front of the wrought iron gates of a castle. This angle emphasized the model's blond-haired pubis, and mini-mized the bartizan in the background, which appeared to grow up from her head like a horn.

"You see the symbolism?" asked Mrs. Desjardins. She had fol-lowed the direction of my gaze. Her bright, interested eyes reminded me of a seagull's eyes, the way it looked at a wrapper or a bit of foil lying on the ground—right before stabbing it.

"Yes," I said.

"Of course you do," said Gil. He spoke without removing his attention from his slate of letters. "These days I find that particular image rather discouraging. I'll leave the deduction to you, George."

The frame was slightly off, and Mrs. Desjardins adjusted it with a finger. "It's obvious, but that's the fun. I mean we're not talking about Immanuel Kant."

"You're embarrassing him," said Gil. "And for God's sake, leave Kant out of this."

"What I mean is we're not talking about rocket science. We're talking about the things that everyone does." Mrs. Desjardins gave me a shrug and a roll of the eyes. She mouthed the word "Grumpy."

I had an odd, uncomfortable feeling; a prickle that started in my stomach and moved up through my chest in waves. This was a sensation I associated with the time when I was small and my mother would go on dates. My grandmother, who often babysat on these occasions, could perceive my growing nervousness as the hours passed. "Stop twitching, Georgie darling. You look like someone just sang Irving Berlin over your grave. She'll be home soon." Now, looking back among the towering German nude, Mrs. Desjardins's too curious eyes, and Gil sitting at the table with whatever it was strapped to his head, I had that same sense of vague but insistent worry.

But in the next moment, the feeling dissipated. I realized that I didn't have time to be worried. I suddenly knew that I needed to go home and try to talk to them. I knew that it was time to apply the principles of collective bargaining.

"Papa said he just wanted a couple of buds if you could spare it. He's kind of worn out."

Gil clucked at his letters. "I sympathize. Believe me. It's going around."

This comment elicited a sigh from his wife.

I stood, resisting the urge to jump from foot to foot. I wasn't a bad kid. I wasn't Steven Sugar. I just wanted to make a point, to have my say. It was like the dream in the mall. If everyone would just slow down, slow down and stop and listen, then I could say what I had say, and—

"The child is waiting, Gilbert," said Mrs. Desjardins.

"Fine," he said. He slid a few letters around his slate.

"Take a look, Dick," said Gil. The old man shifted himself in his wheelchair, pushed up on the armrests, and twisted his body so that the mask of Richard Nixon strapped around the back of his head could see the word on his slate. As always, the disgraced president's expression was arranged in a demented grin, framed by the absurd red bulb of a nose and the wolfish jowls. Gil made a humming noise and nodded his head slightly, which gave the impression that Nixon was thinking it over.

Mrs. Desjardins crossed her arms. "You'll have to excuse him, George. He does this to try and psyche me out," she said. " 'Psyching me out,' he calls it." To my surprise, her sidelong glance appeared to contain a glimmer of real irritation. Then, she sighed and shrugged and chuckled richly. "What a funny old man I have. First, the cancer thing, and now here's Richard Nixon advising him on Scrabble."

With a grunt, Gil dropped back into his chair. "Okay. Dick thinks it's a good idea," he said, and told me to fetch the peppermint tin from the upstairs medicine cabinet. When I came back down, Gil showed me his word: *nascent*. "That's you, kid," he said, and pinched a few dried sprouts onto a cigarette paper.

My grandfather had drifted off again while I was gone, slumped at the window with his mouth agape. With every exhalation a lash of spit unfurled from the tip of his tongue before being abruptly reeled back in the shuddering intake that followed. One of his hands lay clenched in his lap, squeezing a packet of plastic paint-balls into plasma. I pulled the packet loose and set the joint on the windowsill.

When I gave his shoulder a shake, the old man sagged to one side, like a stuffed animal that's gone loose with years. There were peanut crumbs on the front of his shirt. He snorted, but didn't awake.

If he wanted to, Steven Sugar could not only vandalize the bill-board, he could draw horns and a devilish goatee on Al Gore's portrait, then defecate on the lawn, and go goose-stepping around in "le with his lieutenant Tolson marching two paces behind, both of them whooping like Indians and shredding the purloined sections of the *New York Times* and flinging the confetti in the air. He could do all that and more, and I doubted my grandfather would so much as stir.

My need to rush home coalesced into a frank realization: in my mind Steven Sugar was suddenly diminished, and I felt diminished by association, as if we had somehow been allied. Here was an old man in a window, desperate to shoot his enemies with a gun that wasn't even a real gun. Steven Sugar wasn't a fascist; he was just an asshole kid. The thought occurred to me with a kind of amazement. This wasn't a fight; this was pointless.

This accomplishes nothing, I thought to myself. Why does Steven Sugar bother? I looked at Papa, slumped over, the thread of drool now leaking over his unshaven chin. Why does *he* bother? It was like taking something apart, just because you could.

"This accomplishes nothing," I said.

As I lifted him straight in the chair, rearranged his hands, and brushed off the crumbs, I repeated these words aloud to my grandfather, but he was beyond hearing.

14.

On the ride back to Dr. Vic's house the sound of approaching thunder alternated with the slamming of windows against the coming storm, and made me feel as though I were being chased, but that I was winning, that I was ahead.

I tried to think of what I needed to say to them. The breadth of the treaty I was prepared to make astonished me. I felt big and strong lunged. I was going to give them a chance. They would want to hug me; I was willing to let them hug me. They would cry; and I was willing to cry, too. These movements were as plain and clear to me as the things I saw at the far end of the rifle's scope, so clear and so plain that a child or a foolish person might attempt to reach around and touch the magnification with their fingers.

The thickening humidity fell over my shoulders like a wool shawl.

terrorized him for things he couldn't help—for loving my mother, for being a dork—and now he was dead. I killed him.

One of the Laddies emerged from the dock and nudged at Dr. Vic's armpit. He pushed away the dog's nose. The Pekingese gave a whine and trotted away. The dog squatted on the planks and began to shit. Dr. Vic sat up; speared on the end of the dowel was a compact disc. The disc skittered down the dowel and he looked at me with an expression of triumph.

"I got the ice," I said.

"No Jacket Required!" he cried, and shook the compact disc on the stick, like a warrior with a scalp on a lance. "I fucking love this album!"

He was still grinning, glasses streaked with water, when I handed him the tray of ice cubes. "Thanks, George," he said. "I owe you."

The rain was steady now, thrumming off the planks. Dr. Vic sat on the bench and the supports gave a damp creak. He cracked the tray on his knee. I watched him drop a couple of cubes on the deck, and then a couple of more into the tumbler. Soaked through, the heavy material of his orange flannel L.L. Bean work shirt clung to his belly. He splashed in some orange juice and started to pour the vodka. The glass slipped and clattered to the wood. It rolled and bounced swiftly down the planks before flipping off the edge. There was a splash, bubbling. The orange juice on the deck melted away in rain.

Dr. Vic gave a damp snort. His breathing was suddenly thick and emotional.

I glanced away: a good fifteen yards out, I spotted a silver wafer bobbing farther and farther out.

There was a slurping noise, and I turned around to Dr. Vic. He had poured orange juice and vodka into the ice cube tray, and now he was sipping and lapping from the indentations. His eyes blinked at mine over the lip of the tray.

"Have to make do somehow, right?"

"Uh-huh," I said.

"Improvise," he said. "Improvisation."

Dr. Vic sipped his tray, smacked his lips. He smiled at me and gave a sob. I lowered my head to study the dark planks. He breathed, thick and shaky. I could sense the dam about to give way, and the expectation numbed me.

But Dr. Vic started chuckle. The chuckle spilled into a deep laugh, and finally, became a high, wild cackle.

I followed his attention to end of the dock, where the Laddies were hunkered down together, nibbling at a fresh pile of shit.

"You know, George, it seems to me that about the only thing that could be worse than one shit-eating dog, is two shit-eating dogs," said Dr. Vic.

After a few moments, he was able to stop laughing. He cleared his throat and sighed and set his tray down on the bench. His chin trembled.

"George," Dr. Vic said, "I just want you to know that I think you're a super kid. It just didn't work out."

My sneakers carried me down the deck at a run, and I was moving faster when I crossed the lawn, plunging and squishing through the grass, slipping and falling and picking myself up and not even hesitating at the sound of my mother's car pulling up the gravel driveway, not stopping until the sky fell away and a branch stung my forehead, and I was safe in the woods.

15.

For a while, I followed the muddy path with no real idea of where I was headed. I concentrated on the hollow sound of water dripping on the hood of my raincoat. I felt cold and loose-jointed in my clothes. Something about it put me in mind of the Arctic, and the way that hikers sometimes found eighteenth-century explorers frozen on the peaks, perfectly preserved. I pictured my own museum display. "Here is an Ungrateful Child, carbon-dated to the early twenty-first century," a tour guide explained in a nasal tone. "Our studies indicate that this particular specimen ruined his mother's engagement and aided his grandfather in a deranged revenge plot. Very nasty little monster. Died a virgin."

I sat down in wet leaves with my back against a tree. It was near dark and the rain was louder. The ground was cold. I smelled smoke.

They had built a small twig fire in the empty hood of the abandoned Studebaker, and the air almost seemed to itch with the oily smoke from it. The two soldiers sitting in the truck's cab were only faintly visible in the light, but I could see one of them shift to watch me as I approached.

"We had an accident," said Sugar when I came up to the passenger side door. I wasn't afraid.

Beside him, Tolson sat with his head thrown back and his eyes closed. A large purple welt shone on his cheek. What remained of his hair was a scorched mess, and a bloody bald patch lay above his temple. He opened a single eye to look at me, gave two gloomy blinks, and then closed it again.

"Defective flare," said Steven.

"How bad is it?"

"FUBAR," said Tolson. He sounded understandably morose.

"It's not FUBAR," said Steven.

"What's that?"

"He'll be okay after a little R&R."

A gust of rain roared down through the trees, shooting BBs off the roof of the cab. I waved at the damp smoke. Sugar sat as calmly in the front seat as if he were taking a Sunday drive, cruising aimlessly.

"What are you doing now?" I asked.

"Chilling," said Steven.

I nodded. He nodded.

"Wanna come in?" Steven delivered a well-placed heel to the door of the Studebaker and it scrutched open. I said sure and climbed in. They shifted over and Tolson gave a grumble of protest. Steven told him not to be such a pussy. "You just lost some hair, dude."

For a while we didn't talk, just watched the rain rattle the trees. The smoke of the fire billowed from the gaping hood and spilled across the floor of the clearing in tatters. It was dry in the cab, and warm from our shared body heat.

"We've got a bunch of peat logs. We're going to keep it burning all night. Wait out the storm."

"So, you guys hang out here a lot?" I asked.

"Not really," said Steven. "We only set up a camp here recently. When we decided to burn down your house."

I took this in stride. "It's not my house. It's my mother's fiancé's house."

"Well, be that as it may, we were going to raze the fucking thing. Send a message to Old Man McGlaughlin." The bigger boy gave me a frank look. "Your grandfather's attitude has been chapping my ass—big time."

I met the look, shrugged. "Collateral damage, right? That's how it goes. So what happened?"

Steven Sugar grinned. "Tolson fragged himself." He elbowed his partner. "Hey, why don't you try not pointing the flare at your own face next time."

"I'll frag you, you fat prick," said Tolson without opening his eyes.

"Does that mean you're not going to burn down Dr. Vic's house now?" I asked.

"Maybe," said Steven. "The situation is under review." He turned back to the empty windshield. "So what do you do, kid?"

It was the kind of question that wasn't really a question at all, but a challenge. Justify yourself, Steven Sugar was saying, put yourself in the best possible light, impress me. Damp gusts rolled through the trees. Rain pinged dully off the roof.

I thought of my summer: of the hours I spent with Papa, the mission with my mother.

"I'm an activist," I said.

Sugar cast a sidelong glance.

"Activists fight to help people. I want to help people." I used my sleeve to wipe water from my face. "I'm pretty new to it, though."

As night came on, the two boys produced a shopping bag with graham crackers, marshmallows, chocolate, and a single beer. "Don't slobber on the beer," said Steven. We passed it back forth and roasted s'mores until the food was gone and my mouth was rotten and my stomach drum tight.

Steven told me about how he planned to join the army after

graduation. He said he wasn't going in because he was some kind of wannabe asskicker, he just wanted the free ride for technical school. "Not that I'm opposed to kicking some ass, mind you," he said.

I told him I wasn't sure yet, but I was thinking about heading right to college. "Vassar," I said.

Tolson absently plucked blackened tufts of hair from his scalp and cast them in the fire.

We talked until the rain cleared, and the stars came out. Tolson said I shouldn't feel bad about my grandfather. "Mine's crazy, too. He's got that Alzheimer's, and he's, like, obsessed with Sears. Thinks we all work there and nobody is ever waiting on him. He's always like, 'I want some service! I want some service!' Shit bums a guy out." Steven said all his grandparents were dead, but he had a grandaunt. "She's cool. She just listens to the police scanner all day, does a little gardening and whatnot."

A fox strode across the clearing. The creature's eyes glowed green in the dark, and its tail wound in slow circles. We just watched it; no one said anything. The fox disappeared soundlessly into the brush.

We added more peat logs to the fire in the hood. The blaze rumbled higher; sparks wafted into the dark, and died in a blink; the shadows drew long, sober faces across the trees.

"Check this out," I said, and gave Steven a nudge. I removed my shoe, my sock.

Tolson leaned forward to see, too.

I planted my right foot on the ancient dashboard.

"Wow," said Tolson.

"Hey now," said Steven.

"You know what they say about guys with six toes," I said to my new comrades.

I woke at dawn and knew that people were missing me. The other two were still asleep. In the daylight, Tolson's face had a deflated aspect and the coloration of a plum. Steven's snores came in a low consistent rattle, like a generator.

I slipped from the Studebaker and went to piss in the brush. Leaning on a tree, I constructed a plan: I was going to say I was sorry, a lot, to everyone. If I needed to, I would beg. I was going to make everything okay. I had to make everything okay.

Stumbling footsteps carried Steven beside me. "Howdy," he said, and began to urinate.

"I should go," I said.

"Well, don't be a stranger." Steven saluted me with his free hand, and sighed in relief. "And tell your grandfather no hard feelings. Being a paperboy sucked anyway. Tell your grandfather I hope he catches that Nixon guy."

"What?" I asked.

"The guy in the Nixon mask." Steven tucked himself back into his pants. "Tolson and I saw him one night. The guy who sprays shit all over your grandfather's sign."

It took me twenty minutes to jog to the Beachcomber Motel where I stopped to use the pay phone. While I waited I paced the gravel lot. I hoped my father would hurry.

Before this, the last time I talked to Ty Claiborne was on the day of Nana's funeral, at the reception.

I was tired of condolences, tired of thinking. So, I had decided to clean the pool in the backyard, using the net to skim the dead bugs off the surface. That was where I was when my father came out to see me.

"Hey, George," he said. "I wanted to tell you how sorry I am. And that's just for your Nana, for starters."

Ty wore a dark blue suit and sipped a Diet Pepsi while I walked around and around, skimming off the insects, not talking to him. He was a thin, gray man with straw-colored hair. He looked the way I imagined an undertaker should look, drained of blood, sort of dusty. (In fact, the undertaker at Nana's funeral had been a rotund and almost cheerful man, bustling around the funeral home with boutonnieres.)

His appearance had changed a great deal since our previous face-to-face meeting, four years ago, at the incident in the parking lot in Blue Hill. That was when he threatened to kill my mother, and Paul broke his nose with a snow shovel. His hair had been very long then, and he'd lain in the snow, bleeding everywhere, and even after my mother rushed me inside and locked me in the bathroom, I was able to hear him howling.

Looking closer now, I noticed the distinct bump on his nose.

My mother had told me about Ty's two years of sobriety, his new job, the college degrees he earned in prison, and the social work he did at the YMCA. Emma told me how he wanted to talk to me. She said she thought I should. (It was around this time that I had, in fact, stopped speaking to my mother.)

"I know 'sorry' sounds like an excuse, but it's not. It's the fact of the matter. There are no excuses in the program, George. I was a lousy husband and a worse father. I'm an alcoholic and a drug addict and a recovering piece of shit. That's the fact of it. I threw twenty years of my life down a hole and I pelted everybody who looked over the edge with my garbage." He took a deep breath. "And I am sorry. I am so sorry."

Mrs. Desjardins had come out smiling with a garbage bag and collected Ty's Styrofoam cup, then patiently held open the bag as I shook out the net full of dead bugs.

"Nana taught me how to clean the pool," I said to my father when she left.

"Well, then I think that's a fine thing to do today," he said.

We stood around for a couple more minutes, and I didn't say anything else. The pool was clean. Then he tried to give me his phone number. "If you want," he said.

"I'm not taking it unless you promise not to call me," I said.

Ty promised, and kept his promise.

16.

When the taxi pulled up to the curb in front of the Beachcomber, I wasn't thinking about the promise. I was thinking about the island of Rhodes and the article by the divorced professor. I remembered the writer's bizarre notion that the Knights of St. John had transformed into voyeuristic stray cats, basking in the sun and admiring the ripe brown breasts of European tourists. I remembered the cashier at the Citgo, the Goth kid with the fork on his Adam's apple who took so much interest in the Desjardins. "Dammit. Janet."

The wheels of the station wagon crunched over the gravel and I ran from the phone booth.

I threw the door open and dropped into the cracked leather of the backseat. The car smelled like pine and cigarettes.

"Hey," said Ty, "I'm glad you called. You know your mother's looking for you?"

"I need to go to my grandparents' house," I said.

"Are you going to call your mother when you get there?"

"Yes." Then I added, "Please don't talk to me."

"Sure," he said. "Are we in a hurry?"

"Yes," I said.

Ty swung the car around the lot, and onto Route 5. He flicked on the tape deck. Bob Dylan piped up in a honky-tonk clatter. Bob said he couldn't believe it; just last night they had been together, and now she acted like they never had met. The car rolled over a fallen branch in the road, gave a bounce. Without looking around, Ty reached back and pointed at the seatbelt by my shoulder. I pulled it down and locked it.

" 'Dammit. Janet.' Mean anything to you?"

"*Rocky Horror Picture Show*. I projected it."

"Mean anything else to you?" I asked.

"Not unless you really like cross-dressing, or Tim Curry."

"Thanks," I said, still not exactly sure what I was onto, but beginning to feel the edges of it.

"Sure." My father turned onto the interstate. Ty reached back again and made a window rolling gesture. I told him to go ahead. He put down his window. We streaked past a rig pulled over to the shoulder and blinking its hazards; water glistened off the cut granite that walled the road. The morning air was sharp and sweet.

"Do you have a cell phone?" I asked.

"Uh-huh," he said, and passed it back.

I called my grandfather. The phone rang five times and Nana picked up. "Don't mourn, organize," she said, and gave a wheezy chuckle. "And leave a darn message, too." The machine beeped. I clicked off.

The taxi whooshed up the off-ramp, made a left onto Dundee Avenue. I stared at the back of my father's head, his short-cropped orange hair, sprinkled with gray. There were just a couple of more miles before we got to where we were going. I was nervous and afraid and ready. I wasn't really thinking of him as my father. That was a good thing, maybe.

My father was a bad guy; he was an addict and a felon, a wild man screaming and gushing blood in the snow. Ty Claiborne, however, was a middle-aged taxi driver who had given me a lift when I was in a pinch. A guy reached out, you gave him hand—and vice versa.

We slammed to a stop at the curb and I saw Papa lying there on the lawn. I had my seatbelt off and the door of the taxi open before it stopped.

I stumbled forward, pinwheeling my arms for balance, and pitched onto the damp turf. I got up and ran, dropped to my knees beside him.

He was on his back, the tails of his bathrobe spread out in the grass. The breath came from his mouth in a whistle. His eyes were glazed, holding the billboard at a diminishing angle, like the plane of building's façade. There was the grave etching of former vice-president Albert Gore Jr., followed by the bold, true statement:

THE REAL PRESIDENT OF THE UNITED STATES.

But one could not fail to notice what had been scrawled across the legend in green spray paint: **VOTE NADER SHITHEELS!**

"It's going to be okay, Papa," I said. "It's going to be okay." Nothing in his face gave a sign that he heard me. He had eyes only for Al Gore.

I had my father's cell phone. I started to punch the numbers.

"We already called an ambulance," said Mrs. Desjardins.

Gil and his wife were standing there, too, of course.

*   *   *

At that point, I wasn't aware of the details; that Gil had been writing travel articles for obscure newspapers for years (under the pseudonymous name G. T. Flowers); that, typically, he wrote these articles about places he had never visited; that these articles often included references to naked Europeans, stray cats, his ex-wives, and a very few other things that were of lasting interest to him; that he had been so surprised at being accepted for publication in the Sunday *New York Times* that he had been unable to wait the time it would take to drive to the supermarket and instead, rushed next door and plundered the Travel section of my grandfather's delivered copy.

Nor did I yet understand that one of the main reasons Gil had continued to pluck sections from my grandfather's newspaper was simply because he was too cheap to subscribe and too lazy to drive to the Citgo for his own copy; that another reason he didn't like to go to the Citgo was because the manager (he of the fork-tattooed Adam's apple) had once encountered Gil in an entirely different venue: one night at the USM campus movie theater at a midnight showing of *The Rocky Horror Picture Show*, when Gil was dressed in leather chaps with the cheeks cut out, and riding a tricycle up and down the aisles.

Above all else, I couldn't see that the vandalizing of Papa's billboard had nothing at all to do with the Sunday *New York Times* or Steven Sugar. I was not wise to the history of Gil's relationship with Ralph Nader, to the depth of his wild devotion for the man. It was only a few months later—after the filing of Gil's fifth divorce—that we received a letter from Mrs. Desjardins that filled in the final blank:

To put it succinctly, she said that Gil believed with absolute certainty that he had once stroked Ralph Nader's naked thighs at a masquerade orgy. This mystical union had, according to Gil, occurred following a lecture on the applications of Kant to the Watergate scandal at an all-night bash at the Beverly Hills Hyatt in 1973. The man he swore to be Nader had worn a purple Zorro mask, but Gil was nonetheless utterly convinced of the fearless consumer advocate's identity. Furthermore, Mrs. Desjardins wrote (in a manner of phrasing which in no way belied a hint of jealousy), that it was Gil's testimony that the masked man had returned his thigh-stroking in kind, and with all the compassion and attention that one might have expected from a person who had selflessly dedicated his life to the public good.

At least, that was what she said.

But above and beyond such talk, I could never have guessed that Gil—funny old, dirty old Gil—possessed the capacity for the sort of pique which he must have nurtured over the course of the years, as my grandfather carried on and on, about his unions and solidarity and the common good. I could never have guessed at how it must have grated on him.

Which is to say, I didn't know Gil at all.

I gaped at the man. The name Tom Hellweg came to my mind, and just as quickly blew away again, like a bad smell.

Small and frail, Gil stood wearing his wife's kimono, his hands sullenly jammed in the pockets. The Richard Nixon mask sat on top of his bald skull. There was red paint splattered on his neck and on the mask, from where my grandfather hit him with the IL-47, a killshot from the sniper's nest in the guest room.

Mrs. Desjardins wore a pair of leather overalls, elbow-length gloves, and a driving cap emblazoned with a pink swastika. "The ambulance should be right along." She was, as always, smiling brightly. "I think it's just a stroke."

"He wouldn't shut up about the politics," said Gil. "He couldn't take a little teasing."

I said the obvious thing, the only thing that mattered. "You were his friend."

"He never chipped in for any of my grass, either," said Gil.

"You were his friend," I said again.

He worked his hands deeper in the kimono. The Nixon mask sat on his head like a deflated pie.

"And, furthermore, Ralph Nader never owed Al Gore a goddamn thing."

The car door slammed. Ty's shoes beat across the pavement.

The old man in the kimono glanced over with a grimace.

Ty stopped beside me. "Costume party?" he asked.

"That's it. I'm going home," said Gil, and he turned, walked rapidly down the driveway, and disappeared around the hedge in a whisper of silk. Mrs. Desjardins followed him, giggling as she tottered away on her motorcycle boots.

We were alone then, my father and my grandfather and I, on the lawn, the three of us crouched in the shadow of the billboard of the man that should have been president.

"Papa," I said, "Papa, can you hear me?"

His eyes slid slowly over to look at me, like rusted screws being wrenched loose. The skin of his face was slack and ashen. He opened his mouth, but he could only produce a croaking noise.

"Don't talk," I said. I pulled the flaps of his bathrobe closed.

Ty jogged out to the street to wave down the ambulance so they didn't miss the split in the avenue.

Papa stared at me. His eyes were blue and scared. A tear welled and rolled down his cheek, grooving along a wrinkle before falling to the ground.

I grabbed his hand. "You're going to be fine, Papa," I said. I squeezed to show him exactly how things were going to be. "I'm with you. I'm here."

He opened his mouth to speak—and coughed again. There was a hitching noise, a wet clicking, and I could see he was trying to swallow. He started to blink rapidly, deep color filling his cheeks.

This was it; this was the part where my grandfather died.

This was the part before the part where we went to another funeral. I saw the old men in the black vinyl Local 219 jackets lingering at the back of the funeral parlor. I heard them whisper about the time Henry McGlaughlin stuck out his thumb and asked a big-shot defense contractor if he needed any help climbing up on it. I watched us lower another coffin into the ground and heard everyone sing the "Internationale" while the priest stood there looking nervous.

I saw it all, and I felt it.

I still had Ty's cell phone. I dialed home.

*   *   *

"Hello?" I felt a surge of relief at the sound of Dr. Vic's voice.

"I think he's choking," I blurted. "I think Papa's choking."

There was a moment of silence. On the ground, my grandfather's entire body had started to tremble, to vibrate like a tripped wire. His eyes were rolling. I heard the ambulance siren in the distance.

"What makes you think that, George?"

"His face is turning purple. He looks like he's trying to swallow."

"Okay, I believe you—"

"—thank you, I'm sorry," I said.

He cut me off. "Not now—I'm betting that what your grandfather is choking on is a peanut. I want you to open his mouth, and put your finger on his tongue. I want you to get your finger down as far as you can and pull that thing loose."

Papa's mouth was already agape. I plunged my index finger in, stabbing the back of his throat. I hit something hard and dug at it with my nail. In the next instant, he gasped, and chomped down on my finger.

The ambulance whooped to a stop and the EMTs came running across the lawn.

I brought my finger up to my face, and looked at it, and saw it was crooked. I put it down and breathed and lay there. The sun was up over the house, lighting the shingles gold. I lay there some more.

Ty squatted down beside me. "Your mother's on the phone," he said. "She wants to talk to you."

I sat up and nodded at him. He was almost an old man. When I looked at his face, I could see how I would look when I was old. That was okay. We both had time. People live a ton.

"Mom?"

Her voice came in a rush. "Are you okay? Just tell me that you're okay, George. I need to know that you're okay."

I was fine. "I'm fine," I told her, and she gasped, and then we both started talking.

ORGANIZE!

The day the skyscrapers fall we are at the hospital. Papa has been moved into long-term care, where therapists are helping him learn to

*speak and walk again. My mother, Dr. Vic, and I sit around his bed
and watch the television in the corner of the ceiling. We eat our way
through Papa's untouched lunch in shocked silence. The old man's
face is frozen in a lopsided half smile; he always look drunk now. He
doesn't try to speak. None of us does, really. On the television, a
reporter attempts to describe the sound that a human being makes
when it free falls one hundred stories and strikes the roof of an
automobile. This description is inadequate.*

*At some point, the president comes on. He tells us to be calm. He
tells us everything is under control.*

*My grandfather begins to cry. He speaks with a helium voice
through a mouthful of cotton. "The president looks strong, doesn't
he? I think he's going to be okay. I really do." The half smile is
grotesque, and I hate myself for not wanting to look at him.*

Emma turns off the television and goes to him.

"Can I have my Jell-O?" he asks.

"I ate it," I say.

*He sobs. He half smiles. "It's okay, George. They give us all we
want."*

*At their wedding, my mother and Dr. Vic's first dance is to a song by
the Flying Burrito Brothers. If nothing else, I have come to appreciate
my stepfather's solidity, his consistency. He loves comestible bands,
and my mother loves him. I accept it.*

*For their honeymoon in December, the newlyweds tour the islands
of the Mediterranean. I have Christmas with Ty and we go to see Bob
Dylan at the State Theater in Portland. Bob is as spindly as a
grasshopper. "Do you think Bob kind of looks like the Queen of
England?" asks Ty. We seem to get along, my father and I.*

*On the drive home I ask him about his polydactyl toe. He laughs.
He says his fell off the first time he was in rehab. "I found it in my
sock. It just fell off."*

*I don't believe him. But he pulls over and shows me—and it's true.
There's a fine scar at the edge of his foot, nothing more.*

"Did it hurt?" I ask.

"No," he says, "but I miss it."

"Why?"

"Because it was a part of me," he says.

I am the last six-toed man in my family.

We visit my grandfather at the assisted living center where he has been moved. There is an orange zeppelin of a cat that wanders among the infirm and the elderly, and Papa has become the creature's greatest friend. The cat's name is Softball. While we try to engage Papa in a conversation about the weather or the seniors' bowling league, he ignores us and talks to the cat. "Softball would eat any terrorist that tried to kill the geriatrics, wouldn't he? Wouldn't he just kill those terrorists?"

In the halls at school, I nod to Steven Sugar and his former lieutenant, Tolson. They flip me vague salutes. Tolson's face has healed, but one side is dark, as if he is always thinking bad thoughts.

My mother tells me that the Mediterranean was beautiful, and that "yes, the reports of numerous naked breasts being on display in Rhodes were true." She laughs like crazy about that, but I'm embarrassed. So I only let her kiss the top of my head. The last thing she says to me is, "I'm going to be late for work."

My mother and Charlie are locking up the clinic late that afternoon when the rusted blue minivan comes screeching into the parking lot. The GFA woman, the one who likes to scream about whoremasters, and wears a baseball cap emblazoned with a sparkly crucifix, leaps out of the van with a bucket. My mother steps forward, and Charlie fumbles for his gun. The GFA tosses the bucket, drenching my mother in a spray of dirt and earthworms, and then catching her across the mouth with the plastic rim. Emma tumbles to the pavement, and there is the sound of something cracking just right, like an egg on the rim of a bowl. The egg is my mother's skull and the rim is the curb, and in a moment she is gone.

She feels nothing, they say, but no one could know that.

And then, my vision becomes real, and the three men meet at the Beachcomber in their black suits, and my father and Dr. Vic and I

*pick them up. Dale has come in from Boston where he moved with
his new wife and family, and Paul has come from Blue Hill, and
Jupps has traveled from the hydroponic farm in the Netherlands.*

*Jupps presents me with a beautiful tomato that he snuck through
customs. I return his suitcase. "We took it everywhere," I tell him,
and he starts wailing and drops his beautiful tomato in the mud.*

"Man," says Paul in the car, "oh, man."

*"I have been bummed before, but this is brand fucking new. This is
a kick in the nuts to end all kicks in the nuts." Dale unrolls the
window and sticks his head out like a dog. Jupps gives Dale the
tomato and tells him to throw it.*

"I'm sorry very much about that," says Jupps.

*Paul tells him not to sweat it, man. "These things happen, you
know?"*

*Instead of the "Internationale," we sing "Amazing Grace," for
obvious reasons.*

*After the funeral, Myrna Carp insists on speaking with me privately.
She pushes me down on a couch in a dark room. She has mascara all
over her face. She sniffles and cuddles my head against her breasts. It
is her duty, insists Myrna, unbuckling my pants, something she owes
to my mother.*

*"No," I say. "Do you have a condom," I say, and Myrna reminds
me that she's on the pill, but I insist, and on the night I bury my
mother, I ball up my dirty shorts and throw them under the bed. I do
not believe in an afterlife, but I know Emma would be pleased that I
used a condom.*

*I do what anyone would do: cry like I'll never be able to stop. No
one comes to check on me.*

*Three years later, my grandfather has lost interest in the news. It is
unclear how much he remembers, but he likes to pet Softball and to
be wheeled around the grounds of the nursing home. He is sleeping
now beside me, the two of us seated beneath the boughs of an elm
tree. I am home on vacation from my freshman year of college.*

I don't know how I feel about it. I wish someone could explain it, make it all neat and simple, like a ballot. I could just check off a choice, and never worry about free will again.

I wonder where Steven is at this moment. He joined up right after graduation, just like he said he would.

It must be night over there, a night like blue silk over the desert city, and the dust and the sand and the quiet between outbursts.

"Okay," says Captain Sugar. "Okay, men." His troops are gathered around him in a circle. From the wrecked town square there are crooked little lanes running in all directions, pointing a dozen different routes out of the combat zone.

The captain's face is scorched and haggard, but he meets every gaze in turn. "If we work together," he promises, "we can still get out of this mess."

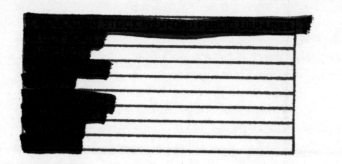